**BLACKPOOL**

PAUL BILIC

# BLACKPOOL

*A Parable*

TAMBURLAINE
2002

First published in 2002 by
Tamburlaine
13 Kilner House
Clayton Sreet
London SE11 5SE

Paul Bilic's right to be identified as the author of this work has been asserted by him in accordance with the Copyright, Designs and Patents Act 1988

Copyright © Paul Bilic 2002

ISBN 0-9541679-0-2

A CIP catalogue record for this book is available from the British Library

All rights reserved. No part of this book may be reproduced or transmitted in any form, electronic or mechanical, including photocopy or any information storage and retrieval system, without permission in writing from the publisher.

Typeset in Garamond 12/13pt
from the author's disk by Scriptmate Editions

Manufacture coordinated in UK by Book-in-Hand Ltd
20 Shepherds Hill  London N6 5AH

## Contents

- 7   Chapter One: Prague Days
- 22   Chapter Two: The Ace of Spades
- 41   Chapter Three: Mandryka
- 60   Chapter Four: Randy and Lucky
- 73   Chapter Five: Style Lord Gentleman
- 87   Chapter Six: The Counting House
- 106   Chapter Seven: The Metropole
- 126   Chapter Eight: Our Kind of Laughter
- 150   Chapter Nine: A Redistribution of Patrimony
- 165   Chapter Ten: The Bluff Way

## Chapter One: Prague Days

THERE IS great fun to be had by turning a toad onto its back and poking it around with a pointy stick. In much the same way a foolish oaf humiliated by lighter, cheerier characters can be the source of enormous pleasure. This is wicked wisdom.

Patak—our toad—steps out of his bedroom into the broad wash of light falling in through the drawing room window. This is his apartment on the teeming Lenski Ave, Prague; an apartment about as large as his personality, big enough with just a hint of the superfluous.

He opens up the window and dares to lean out. It is snowing. Flanking the window on the facade of the block is a huge caryatid angel. Patak peers into the foot-high eyes of the guardian. He looks across over the smoking chimney pots and spinning weather vanes beside the calm gaze of the angel and feels like a king surveying his lands.

The tableau fades to grey.

Now here is Patak sleeping the sleep of the just. His bed is worth a word or two because it is not really a bed. It is a mattress on top of a door on top of a gutted chest of drawers. He did not know where the door came from as he had bought the set (mattress, door and shelves) from a newspaper ad (*selling all furniture due to sudden departure for Latin America*), but he sometimes thought of that door (in his irritating, childlike way) as the door to the other side of his life.

Patak sleeps on.

Another scene is coming now. Patak on the red tram travelling through Prague. Patak liked Prague. There were parts of it he loved and knew intimately, dark quarters he liked to know the existence of but thought were best left alone, streets that bored him, places (squares or avenues) where he liked to linger. Here on the tram, for example, is the slight swerve of the Avenue Klaster as it crosses over the crossroads of Avenue Tepu and begins skirting the Karlov Gardens on the left, leaving behind the dome of the observatory which, when you peer out of the back window of your tram, becomes a head clambering to get a look in at the window. When the tram suddenly accelerates to take the slight curve and ease through the lights, an amalgam of memories and sensations jostle in Patak's head, which together take on the form of that easy swinging sensation in his stomach coming from the buoyant acceleration of the tram at that moment.

In the tram Patak plots the points of his Prague compass: South is his work zone; West is the University and the cafés looking onto the Karlov Gardens; East is the hotel where his mother had stayed years ago when she had come to visit him. North, where the tram is bound, is home, the conquered territory, the bars he knows, the restaurants, his apartment, his table and chair, his bed, his caryatid angel.

At this stage we become aware that there is a box in the corner of the frame portraying another scene. Here are our lighter, cheerier figures. Still in hibernation, they have not yet been called upon to turn Patak over onto his back. Electricity has not yet fizzed them into animation. For the moment they are sleeping in their box, so we shall have to stay with cumbersome Patak.

That was just to let you know.

Now cut back to Patak pleasantly cavorting in the hills and dales of his life.

Girlfriends. He had been acquired and shed by girlfriends at regular intervals. Dominique, who had first defined for him his irritating, childlike manner so that it was now lodged in his own mind and he waited for the moment when other girlfriends would start to get their inklings of it. Doris, the breastless redhead. Tanja the Catholic who clicked into furious sexual action when the light went out, so that he sometimes wanted to surprise her by clicking the light on again to check it was really the same person. Audry, the freckled skater, who had left him for a so-called artist whose a.r.t. consisted (it seemed to Patak) of making up puns for scraps of material cut into the shape of rag persons. e.g. Polly Esther. Vanina whom he had left (she was too short for him; when they stood kissing on the open street—he cringed just thinking of it—he had to stoop. Ugly! Ugly! ) They were all up there now, like a set of paper dolls, lodged in the dress circle of his mind, out of harm's way.

Job-wise the list went like this: stationery clerk; documentalist's assistant; junior picture editor on a daily newspaper; Chief Picture editor on an insurance weekly. Those were the main ones. As picture editor on the insurance paper, he dealt in snaps of granitic-jawed insurance executives, ships under construction and cats. Cats were his principal type of photograph. All kinds. Natural cats, many of them life-threatening, and cats that came about due to negligence on the part of the insured. Hurricanes, tornadoes, tidal waves, forest fires and droughts; motorway pile-ups and terrorist bombings, aeroplane crashes and broken legs. All kinds of catastrophes. Cats were his bread and butter. He wrestled with tornadoes and tidal waves every day and was pleased to get back home to his ordinary apartment on the Lenski Avenue in one piece.

One thing that Patak had never acquired was a good idea, the kind of idea that makes your heart strings twang. But one day, a summer's day in the Mala Strana, the western quarter of Prague over the river where the poor were parked and life was cheap, Patak suddenly came up trumps. It was an idea for a game show for the T.V. He had just been looking at an electronic poster for the latest game show entitled Rooks and Pawns which was due to start that very evening and he started to imagine how such a game show might be. But what he imagined had nothing to do with your average run-of-the-mill game show and was, moreover, nothing like the actual Rooks and Pawns when he viewed it at 7.30 that evening. No, his imaginary game show was quite different.

In his game show of the mind the studio audience stood to gain by the defeat of the contestant. Think on. If the contestant got the question wrong or failed the task the studio audience shared out the winnings amongst each other. If the contestant succeeded in his task, the studio audience went away empty-handed. Not a complex idea but the germ of a great one, thought Patak. Adversarial instead of supporter games; interactive instead of passive. You saw it in the sport's stadiums where hatred played as large a role as support. What had to happen now was for it to be brought into the T.V. studio. Add a studio audience selected from the lower echelons, by which one meant west of the river Mala Strana way, and hey presto, a brand new genre, original merchandise.

Every evening after work Patak elaborated a new nuance into the mechanics of his game show until after a few weeks he had built it up into a whole sub-culture and was already imagining its cult following and his own fame management.

The idea struck Patak as he was making his way down towards the Karluv Bridge that would take him from the Mala Strana back to the familiar Old Town, where he lived. He had crossed the river into the Mala Strana to pick up some beans from his favourite bean supplier, and as he wended his way down the dusty mid-afternoon street, a raggedy young man crossed in front of him.

—Good Afternoon, sir, cried the fellow.

Patak nodded by way of a greeting.

—Where are you headed so fast? asked the scallywag.

—I'm crossing back over into the old town, answered Patak, keeping up his pace. This was after all the Mala Strana, not exactly the safest place in Prague.

The young fellow took up a marching step beside him imitating the tread of a grenadier.

—May I accompany you? he asked after a moment.

—It seems to me you already are, said Patak. Perhaps, he thought, if he simply ignored the man, he would leave him alone. But as they approached the bridge, the young man was still with him.

—I take it you do not live in the Mala Strana, said the young man after a moment.

—No, answered Patak, eyeing his companion for the first time. How do you reach such a conclusion?

—Simple. The way you dress, the way you hold your head, your accent of course, and even the way you walk.

Patak stopped. The bridge was in sight now and there was no threat.

—Well, you're right, he said. I have an apartment to the north of the Old Town. But I must say I'm impressed by your qualities of observation. And you, I suppose you live in the Mala Strana?

He was not sure if he was trying to be rude or not, but he knew his voice betrayed him. He sounded curious.

The young fellow smiled.

—Guess, he said.

—I would say that you were, said Patak.

—And why might you think such a thing? asked the young blackguard.

—Oh, I don't know, those things you mentioned the other way round, I suppose. But also, why should you take such an interest in the other side of the river if you weren't. And, moreover, here we are in the Mala Strana, it makes sense that you live here.

The young man smiled again.

—Well, I am actually in the process of moving from the Mala to the other side, so I suppose you could say that for the moment, I am a mixture of both.

Patak looked into his face for an instant. He was not as young as he had first imagined. Perhaps the fellow was no more than a year or two his junior. His keen eyes were a vivid china blue and his cheeks were rosy. He had a friendly look to him and, with no more than his quaint Mala Strana locutions as evidence of character, Patak believed he could trust him.

They marched on abreast for a minute until Patak caught sight of the bridge up ahead. A light was on in the constable's cabin, so Patak looked in his breast pocket for his identity card.

—Yes, well, I'll be bidding you good day, said the fellow and had quickly about-turned to make his way back into the Mala Strana. In a moment he had hurdled over a fence and was gone.

Patak walked home brooding. He knew he ought to feel relieved. The man was clearly a pest and probably wanted by the authorities to judge by the way he had hurdled that parapet. Yes, clearly a nuisance of some sort or other, but for some reason Patak felt a sense of loss. He hadn't even found out what the young man wanted.

Patak's present girlfriend was called Julia. He had met her in the street when the bottom fell out of her paper bag of plums and he had stooped with her to help her pick them up. What had happened then was not that moment on T.V. commercials when she gets a whiff of his after shave or he gets a nose of her perfume and hence unspeakingly consents to love him (or he her, depending on the product). No, it had not happened like that. They just picked up the plums and that was that. But, as fate would have it, they were bound for the same underground station and so were compelled to walk together and stand on the same platform, which made it difficult for them not to exchange looks, leading to smiles, and words, and so on and so forth, the bob sleigh round of phone numbers, calls, coffees, dates, uncertainties, resolutions, arguments and—eventually—boredom. Now they had completed the course and were ready to call it a day. Now and again they would beat it out in an oblique and tortuous argument. Open dissent and fury were reserved for practical events of particular and restricted incidence: if ever she left the tap dripping, not turning the faucet tightly enough; if ever he flicked his hair back in that irritating and childlike way of his.

There had been highlights: sharing a phone receiver in a winter phone booth; an outdoor performance of Ben-Hur with the amplified soundtrack booming into the sultry August night; kisses on a railway bridge in the autumn. But the deep underlying problem was that she just couldn't get it into her thick skull that his present life was a temporary and unimportant stage on the way to the real thing, which was going to take place when he got his game show idea accepted by the powers-that-be.

It wasn't as if Patak hadn't treated her to a serious exposition. One day as she came out of the bathroom after having applied one of her night creams, he confronted her. He was wearing his orange Y-fronts at the time.

—Freeze, he told her. Freeze. He pointed an imaginary gun at her.

He paused for a moment to let the tension settle, then he started up:

—Antagonism Game Shows: A New Concept in Viewer Participation. For a Game show of the Future...

This was an extract from his written proposal, where he spelt it all out in full. The exact function of the Game show host and his two assistants or as he called them the Director of Operations and the two Agonists. The participants were called Protagonists and the audience Metaprotagonists. The whole dramaturgy was spelt out in those terms with different parts of the set coloured in terms of their dramaturgical weight. The set was littered with a range of accessories: glass booths like ducking stools; sitting zones like stocks and pillories; roulette wheels like racks, so that the set looked like a torture chamber. Patak gave the set the name of the Game Chamber.

Anyway, between the hours of midnight and one in the morning Patak laid it all out for her. Julia just sat there on the eiderdown while it sank in, the night cream that is. From time to time she nodded, from time to time pursed a lip, from time to time raised an eyebrow. It wasn't much of a reaction.

—We'll discuss it tomorrow, she said.

Patak was looking about for someone who might help him to bring this project to the surface. He spoke to Julia the next day. He told her he was thinking of giving up his job to devote his time to finding supporters for his project. He had some savings, he had never been a great spender. How much did he have stowed away now? Enough to keep him for two or three years if he tightened his belt. But Julia didn't like the idea. He knew immediately from how her mouth seemed to get thinner as he was speaking to her (she must have been holding her breath to let him finish and give the impression she was listening to him reasonably). No, it was nonsense. Why couldn't he just grow up? He should have got these illusions out of his system years ago. It was ludicrous for him to be still lugging this kind of nonsense around with him. After all, how old was he now? Thirty eight. Thirty eight. He was supposed to be a grown-up. Thirty-eight-year-olds were running the world. Did he realise that? Exactly. This was his chance to make it big, to get in on power. Julia laughed. Julia laughed so that he saw her numerous and efficiently planted silver fillings glisten like a trapful of treasure.

Here now is Patak pushing open the great wooden doors of the Central Prague Television Network Building on Republiky Square with the firm intention of obtaining an appointment with Jerzy Grotowski, head of the network's light entertainment department. The girl behind the reception desk smiled engagingly but insisted there could be no meeting without an appointment and no appointment without a stamp from the Television Authorities Committee.

Patak knew about the Television Authorities Committee. His request for an appointment with them was still being considered five months down the line. They held what they referred to as a surgery for the general public once a week and applications to attend figured on a list the length of Wenceslas Square. What Patak really needed was not to be a member of the general public, that charmless block of the population that he yearned—yes, yearned with his entire pang ridden soul—to abandon.

As Patak pleaded with the smiling receptionist—and, by the way, Patak was old enough to be her father—his eyes fixed on the poster for the new T.V. game show produced by the network stuck up behind the reception desk. Foolish Thoughts, game show mania produced by Jerzy Grotowski and the light entertainment crew. Patak had seen the first programme last week. It was junk. Contestants attempted to participate spontaneously in a staged five minute drama and attain the mystery prize at the end. Depending on how they managed to orientate the action the prize ended up more or less valuable. Last week's prizes were a motorcycle, a goldfish in a bowl and a kilo of carrots. At the end of the show the woman who won the carrots applauded and laughed joyfully as though she had got the star prize, which went to show what a hoax the whole thing was. Did she want to win the carrots or did she want the motorcycle? The whole premise of the show was that she was mildly indifferent to what she won and that the only thing she really cared about was competing. Now, in sport that notion had gone out with the ark. These days sportsmen admitted that they were out to win. It was time gameshows were based on the same honesty, and then perhaps real drama might enter the arena. And as to where the foolish thoughts of the title came in, that was anybody's guess. The marketing gurus would have thought the title up months before even seeing the show.

They would have costed it, locked it in and shipped it out, partnered it with press outlets, given it a profile, packaged it, advertised and merchandised it, sold and contracted it, indexed it to the appropriate sections of the population, vaunted it, elevated it, condemned it and pathologised it, all before the sparrow-brained 'ideas-man' had even thought about what the show would actually be.

Zounds, thinks Patak as he shuffles out the network building, his lank strands of thinning hair flapping into his eyes as he encounters the wind of the great outdoors. He is a slight figure in the huge institutional doorway. Patak 'out and about', to coin a weatherman's expression. As far as the furtherance of his gameshow ambitions were concerned, these futile sorties were as good as it got.

It was a couple of weeks after these initial setbacks that Patak met up with an old acquaintance in The Golden Stag. The Golden Stag was his favourite bar: in recent weeks he had taken to frequenting it more and more, which meant perforce that he was seeing less of Julia. It was in the Golden Stag that Patak was wont to turn his mind round the subject of that shimmering and all-inclusive edifice which was his Game Show idea—to call it an idea was absurd, it had become an inner maze where Patak rooted around, a homely and friendly maze with padded walls and a domestic biscuity smell.

Patak had been in the saloon bar for a number of minutes dreaming up new twists to the game show concept, when a stranger brusquely snapped into his field of vision and smiled. Now that his features animated Patak recognised him immediately. The merry blackguard from the Mala Strana.

—Randy Hart, said the stranger, holding out his palm.

—I beg your pardon.

—The name's Hart. Randy Hart. I'm happy to see you again, sir.

—Patak.

They shook hands on it.

—I vowed that if ever I met the amiable fellow from the bridge, I'd shake his hand, and more than that I'd buy him a drink.

The stranger was dressed in what amounted to a collection of rags. The hand that Patak shook was wearing an old pair of fingerless gloves and when the young man made his way along the bar towards Patak he picked up a bulky round sack which contained (Patak was willing to wager) the extent of his worldly possessions.

—No, said Patak. This one's on me.

Patak stood the round.

—You're a gentleman, said Hart.

When they were sipping their dark beers together, Hart took up in earnest:

—I'll come to my point. When I told you I was moving from the Mala Strana to the Old Town that day on the Karluv Bridge, I perhaps failed to mention that in so doing I was planning a wholesale change, of lifestyle, of accent, of expectations. In short, I was moving to a world where the notion of success has a meaning. Not, perhaps, a world where the notion exists for me at the present moment. Maybe you've guessed. I have not yet made the grade.

Hart lifted his palms up and away from his body, as if to say, take me, take me as I am, poor and forked etc.

—So what's your scheme? asked Patak.

—Thank you for asking, sir. Thank you for asking. You don't know what that represents to a man such as myself. Coming from the west of the river as I do, the Old Town residents immediately take the view that such schemes as I might have will necessarily be of little worth. But a man can dream, can he not? A man can strive.

—True enough, agreed Patak and savoured a mouthful of beer.

—You yourself must have dreams of your own. Even a man as outwardly successful and polished as yourself can dream of attaining another plane, not necessarily better, but different. Such is human nature. We always seek what we do not possess.

—How true. How true.

—Look at me. West of the river a man of substance. East of the river a nobody.

Hart again hoisted those palms up. It had not seemed to Patak that the fellow had been a man of substance, as he termed it, even west of the flood, but, who was he to know? If an outsider caught sight of him, Patak, chatting to this rascal in this bar tonight, would that outsider know that he was hatching an idea that would revolutionise the world of light entertainment as we know it? Men's hearts were not worn on their sleeves.

—My scheme, went on Hart, has not yet taken form. I await the idea which I can believe in one hundred and ten percent and for which every sinew of this body will toil.

—It's true, said Patak. Ideas are what come sparse at our time of life, when we have savoured youth and rejected foolishness.

Hart warmed to this ready wisdom.

—There speaks a man who has drunk deep of life's cup.

Patak made a silent push with the corner of his mouth to acknowledge Hart's judgement with due modesty.

—Perhaps you have a scheme of your own, dared Hart.

Patak took another sip of beer.

—Not quick to answer, eh? I like that, I like that. A man who doles his wisdom out on canapés. And besides, a serious man with a creative project is seldom interested in blabbing. One, why should he let another in on it? Two, he has enough serious selling to do without it cluttering up his leisure. Three, here is not the time or the place.

The fellow was sharp—Patak found himself agreeing with all three of his points—and merited a slight incline of his head and, yes indeed, another beer. How had he gulped that first down so quickly? He had hardly stopped yapping since they met.

—Thank you for the beverage, sir, came the fellow. He was belting it down already, his Adam's apple going like the clappers and the dark liquid lurching lower in the up-turned glass.

—Mr Hart, came Patak. I see you are a quick and eagle-eyed young man. You will therefore appreciate, as you already did in point number three of your list, that here is neither the time nor the place for such confidences.

—Here is the time and the place to make better acquaintance, however. Am I right?

Patak smiled.

—Would this be your local watering hole, sir?

—Local no, but it has become habitual.

—Indeed, said Hart, looking bigger and inclining over the bar towards Patak.

—It has become the place to which I take my thoughts.

—Take them? Carry them carefully no doubt, not wishing them to spill.

Patak had to admit it, the fellow had a way with words and could almost read his thoughts.

Patak nodded:

—An apt and happy image, Mr Hart. Yes indeed. Carefully like a brimful of beer or a babe in arms.

—You do have an enterprise, do you not? An enterprise of moment. Am I right? Am I right?

Patak sipped at his beer and only then deemed fit to acquiesce:

—I flatter myself to think so much.

Randy Hart laughed and swayed his nearly empty glass up to Patak's as though to clink to a common enterprise. But for the moment the enterprise, whatever it was, was not common.

—Then let's rejoice and relax in these your scant moments of distraction.

Now they did clink glasses and drink together.

Patak paid for another round. As he was receiving his change Hart eyed the Old Town currency wedged into his host's thick wallet. Patak felt a sense of power, a sense of having this very specific project nestled within himself. And here was a willing audience. Why not sound out his scheme on eager ears for once? After all, he had met Hart on the very day he had formulated his scheme. He turned to face Hart.

—May I point out one thing before I proceed? These moments, which you call moments of relaxation away, or so you imagine, from the fiery furnace of creative activity, are for me the most productive and creative instants in the day. They are the moments, now running into minutes, when the project that I harbour is chewed on, swilled around. In a word, deliberated and made richer. Precious moments...

—...Which I in my clumsy way have disturbed. Please forgive me.

But Patak stayed his new found companion and, patting him on the back, took up his glass to clink. The clink this time going the other way, then; initiated by Patak and warmly, one might even say affectionately, mirrored by Randy Hart.

For Patak, this was encouragement enough. He began to blab.

## Chapter Two: The Ace of Spades

LIFE IN Prague can be refined, sedate, charming, intense, maddening, defenestrable even, but given its history, given its architecture, given its political topography, given its matt finish, can it ever be as shiny as life in, say, Blackpool, Blackpool England.

Just a thought.

The next day Patak was sitting at home poring over his copy of Lives of the Great Romans Volume II. It was a tome he liked to pull down off the shelf when he was settled for an afternoon in, with the rain lashing the window pane and the wind buffeting up and down the Lenski Avenue. He was wearing clean underwear beneath a nice pair of brown cords to set off a crisp white cotton shirt, and he'd found himself a nice spot at the end of his sofa; it was a dark pink sofa which ran to different shades depending on the way you stroked the weft. Patak occupied no more than two thirds of one of its three ample cushions. It was built to seat three men of enormous bulk and Patak was a mere stripling at 11 stone ten, but he loved to feel the stretch of its emptiness beside him, knowing it could support him in any circumstance, supine singular or supine plural with some companion, Julia for instance, although they usually sat each at one end with their respective backs supported by the thick bolster at the sofa arms, facing each other with their legs stretched out past the other, so that they might massage or tickle one another's feet, should the fancy take them.

Patak was sat up straight on the sofa with his feet planted firmly on his Persian rug that illustrated the rabbit hunt at some outpost of the Persian Empire in bygone days; Lives of the Romans was open on his knee at the woodcut of some particularly noble Roman chieftain pleading before the Senate to be granted the legions to rid one of Rome's provinces of some Barbarian tribe or other, the Visigoths probably. Patak was just about to turn the tracing paper that protected the plate to get a better look at the warrior's noble features and then to advance to the fictionalised text of this largely fictionalised Roman figure when the door bell rang.

Julia used to spend most Saturday afternoons with him but in recent weeks she hadn't bothered stopping by, preferring to spend her time shopping with her girlfriends at Kotva near the Powder Tower or at one of the newer department stores in the renovated Jewish quarter. It was true that whether Julia was there or no, Patak didn't like to miss the Sparta Prague match on the radio, and whatever they were up to together, supine facing each other or supine and stretched out one beside the other on the pink sofa, by three o'clock it had to be finished so that Patak could tune into the sports channel and settle down with a pot of tea and a plateful of delicious Prague gingers. Julia had tried to take an interest in the match at first but she didn't understand football and the radio commentary left her none the wiser. So Patak was mildly surprised and irritated to see her standing under the porch sheltering from the rain and shaking her umbrella out. After all it was two thirty five. The Sparta Prague players would be limbering up in the dressing room already.

—I popped into Kotva on the way over from Lenski's, said Julia, opening up one of her department store bags and pulling out a dress. She lay it out on the pink sofa and looked up at Patak.

—What do you think?

She picked it up and held it against her, looking across to Patak to gauge his reaction. It was a little black cocktail dress. How many little black cocktail dresses did she have, and when did she last go to a cocktail party?

—Very nice.
—Do you think so?
—How much was it?
—On sale. The shop assistant said it was in from Paris and they won't be getting any more deliveries.
—So why was it on sale?
—Winter fashion. In winter they sell summer wear; this is January.
—Good. So it's a bargain?
—A snip. Are you worrying about the football?
—No. Is it that time alread? faked Patak.
—Don't worry. I won't be long. Now look at this.

Julia took out a large ribboned box and sat down on the sofa:
—Take that dusty book off the cushions. How many times have I told you?

She picked up the Lives of the Romans Volume II and dropped it down on the Rabbit Hunt rug:
—What do you think of this?

By now she had taken it out of its box and was trying the hat on. It was a nineteen twenties style hat with an upturned brim at the front, faun in colour with a dash of scarlet.
—I'm wondering if I'm supposed to wear it cockily on one side or straight across. If I wear it cocky I lose the brow line, but if I wear it straight it's a bit too head-on. What do you think?
—Hats are supposed to be head-on, aren't they?
—In a way.
—I don't know. Depending on the day, you wear it either way.
—I mean, what do you think?
—How much was it?
—You don't want to know that.
—No sale this time then? It must be winter wear.
—Hats don't obey the same rules.

Julia had gone off across the room to the mirror and was checking on her silhouette. Patak darted a glance across to the clock on the mantelpiece. Three o'clock; kick-off time.

—Or maybe I should wear it like this?

Now she had turned it through ninety degrees and pulled it down heavily over her eyes. She was peering from under the new-found brim.

—I look like a lady spy.

—Mmmm, said Patak: I'll put the water to boil, shall I?

—No, wait a minute. I bought something else.

Julia strode back over to the sofa and produced a flimsy black undergarment from out of one of the carrier bags.

—I wanted you to see me in it. It's a new nightie. Do you like it?

—Mmm, said Patak in a not-sure scrawl up and down an octave.

In a trice she had disappeared into the bedroom. Patak replaced his Lives of the Romans on the bookshelf. He looked out of the window. Down below on the street a man in grey with what looked like an enormous head was trying to control an umbrella the wind had turned inside out. He tussled with it whilst trying to keep his hat on.

—By the way, Julia shouted from the bedroom. I've got tickets for the opera for tomorrow night. Picque Dame. The Queen of Spades.

Patak's heart sunk again.

He watched the man twirl in his raincoat as he reached over and switched on the radio.

*—Jarmusch to Bokits. Bokits looking to move forward now from deep inside his own half. He pushes a square ball out to the flank just below us here in this brand new stadium. A big crowd in here today. Fifteen thousand. The ball's gone out of play beneath us. Nestroy leaves it to Bokits who sends a long one down the wing. The sun's coming out from behind some*

*angry clouds now. The surface is difficult. It rained a few minutes before the kick-off. A heavy downpour, left the pitch slippery. There's the odd puddle scattered about, especially round the goal mouths. The Racing goal mouth in particular. There's a big puddle on the penalty spot there. Sparta will be hoping for a penalty at the other end. If they get one that is. Nestroy is chasing back now. Has he got the legs? The Sparta Prague midfield are streaming forward. But there's Paleolog running up a dead alley.*

—You can come in now, called Julia from the bedroom.

Patak took a last melancholy look at the man in the raincoat and clicked off the radio.

—But wash your hands first, added Julia.

That was the Sparta match up the spout, supposed Patak.

In fact Sparta won 3–1 with a strike from Paleolog the Pole on the half-time whistle and two penalties in the second period, one of them controversial. A consolation goal for Racing F.C. came two minutes from time, which was enough to upset Sparta's goal difference and leave them in second place behind their rivals Bohemians F.C. No matter. The season was still young.

As far as Patak was concerned, the problem with Julia was that she really didn't comprehend what he was all about. After they had completed their afternoon love-making, she started going on about what she hoped to do next summer. She said there was a new resort in England that was suddenly all the rage; very chic, they were calling it the Monte Carlo of the Irish Sea. Blackpool, it was called. What they could do is they could go there by plane, spend a week on the coast soaking up the sun followed by a week's tourism, trips to interesting spots (there must be some!), cinema and opera, tea shops and string quartets. She adjusted the pillows under their heads and tugged her nightie back into the symmetry from which Patak had tugged it. There was a hotel that her friend Idil had recommended to her. Now what was its name? She had the card at home somewhere. Why didn't they fix the dates now? Patak knew how tricky it was to get them if you didn't put your offer in at work soon enough. How about late May? What was the name of that blessed hotel?

—I wouldn't get your hopes up too high, countered Patak, when he could get a word in.

—What do you mean? Don't you think it sounds romantic? Blackpool. It sounds like a mysterious fairy tale forest land with clear pools and aching sea-scapes.

—Well, it sounds nice enough but you never know what might happen between now and then.

—Like what?

—Anything could happen. You know what life's like?

—I don't know as I do know what life's like.

—Evidently not, came Patak, stressing the *dent* with a solid clash of tongue on palate.

Julia supplied Patak with a slow burn.

—Are you driving at something in particular?

—I'm just saying.

—Why do I always have to guess at what you're saying or bully it out of you? It's no crime to have an idea, you know. Some girls like surprises.

She nuzzled up to him.

—All I'm trying to say is that life's not all holidays.

—I know it's not; four weeks a year. The remaining forty-eight I work. And so do you, Patak. Still, I take it you're not keen on the idea. I should have known.

Patak pulled the bedclothes back and strode out across the bedroom towards the study, his buttocks crumpled and somehow ruefully looking back at her. Julia hated it when he went into his study, and as he crossed the threshold and those buttocks disappeared from sight, she knew what it was all about. Over the last hour in all the fun of thrashing about in the bed she had forgotten about this madcap scheme of his. She heard him shuffling about at his desk and the bleak memory of what had benighted the last few months of their life arose like some direful huge tower block screening out the sun. His Quiz show idea. The merciful saints!

—Come back to bed, Patak, she cooed.

—No. You rest, if you like.

—I don't need to rest. Come on. Don't stay in there. Come back here to me. I'll give you a foot massage.

It really made him cringe when she talked like that. In love-making Patak didn't like talk. He liked to get on with it, enjoy it and then go about his business. It actually invigorated him for his business, if he emerged at the right moment. And yet, outstay the welcome of that right moment and you could kiss invigoration good-bye. It was all a question of cycles.

Julia heard the depressing little note—a silly protracted F with a kind of fuzzed amplification—that indicated his computer was up and running. Julia breathed out and looked across the room to her black knickers on the carpet in the corner where they had been tossed minutes earlier.

—Why don't you have a shower and make us all a nice cup of coffee? came Patak's voice after a moment of tapping around on his computer keyboard.

He clicked into the window of the file marked Antagonism and out fled the four documents: Letter (a draft of an initial approach letter to television producers); Ins and Outs (the actual rules and regulations of his Antagonism Game show as they had so far been elaborated); Contacts (the list of people he had to get to see or who at the very least had to receive letter); and Budget (budget was empty, he didn't know about that side of the affair, it would have to wait until he found a partner). Patak heard the bath running and the bathroom door close. He clicked into Ins and Outs and went to the end of his document. He typed up an asterix and opposite wrote:

> *Must find a way of bringing genuine antagonism into the audience response, emotive antagonism like in football matches, hatred is roughly the right word for it. Audience members may wager different personal possessions against the contestant: items of furniture perhaps, even cars or apartments in the best of cases. Let audience members always receive a number of free tickets so that they are accompanied by family members. Family members will show the range of emotional responses to catastrophe or triumph when the time comes. Mala Strana people are of course the correct sample audience for the most efficient enactment of Antagonisms.*
>
> *Everybody must play a part in the system. Even the Quiz master, who will have his own elaborate stake—his job, no less—tied up in the network. The Quiz master, as much as the contestants, is on the slippery slope that could lead to disaster.*
>
> *The game itself will be bigger than any one personality.*

In general, Patak didn't go west of the river to the Mala Strana. He had always lived east of the river. His father had held a stable post at the state bank, which guaranteed a good enough income at the time to be valid for residence in an East Bank apartment. There were just a couple of distributors south of the river that Patak frequented: the bean shop he had visited on the day of his fortuitous meeting with Randy Hart, and a particularly inexpensive spice merchant. Otherwise he never set foot there, and he certainly never ventured West after dark. One heard such stories. Patak even had a morbid fascination for some of them. The accounts relayed by The Secret Eye magazine which Patak now and again picked up at the newsagents beggared the imagination. *Woman found with nipples chopped off and rammed down her ears; Street gang wrecks every house on a street of two hundred homes; Man's eyes cut out for supporting Sparta Prague* (over the river west-side Star Prague were the local team). No wonder Randy Hart had needed to get out.

There were only two streets that Patak knew west of the river: the main High street, or what he presumed was the main high street, which continued the line of the Karluv Bridge, and a little side street that led off it about three hundred metres into the Mala Strana. The bean shop was on the High street and the spice merchants on the side street, a certain Lodski Ulica. Patak remembered the name as he had once seen a reference to it in The Secret Eye. What troubled Patak, of course, was that he was immediately recognisable as an east-banker. Clothes, bearing, speech: if he opened his mouth, he had the Narodni quarter written all over him.

In Patak's imagination the Mala Strana was a vast creeping grid of evil alleyways interspersed with spice merchants, bean shops and embittered West Bank activists who would cut your throat at the drop of a hat. Julia actually refused to venture west of the river at all. In her entire life, or so she maintained, she had set foot in Mala Strana only once, and that was on faculty trip study day on historical Praha, where she had been chaperoned and surrounded by an assembly of protective and supervisory personnel. So much for Mala Strana and Julia. Which was perhaps a contributing reason why the area held a certain fascination, albeit purely academic, for Patak.

It would in fact be true to say that the Mala Strana was the theatre of Patak's fantasies, not specifically sexual, but, knowing the substitution that had taken place between the Old City and Patak's lack of a long-term sexual partner and confidante, it might be unwise to immediately disclaim any such relationship. The Mala Strana was a patch of his brain as yet unexplored; dark and shadowy perhaps, but in a way seductive, a dark delight stored up for later. When Patak let his imagination race and he thought of Randy Hart as a genuine Mala Stranite, the thought gave rise to a fascinated abhorrence. It excited him.

As operas went Pique Dame wasn't such a bad one. It told the story of a certain Hermann, played by the long-haired baritone with the jowls that Julia had dragged him along to see on countless occasions. Anyway, in this particular story he was addicted to gambling and heard of a magic sequence of cards known by a spooky old Countess which she had been told of by the devil or someone and which when used could secure your fortune.

Anyway, to cut a long story short, the spooky old Countess snuffs it when Hermann's trying to wring the magic sequence out of her scrawny old neck. Tri Karti he keeps saying to her. Tri Karti Tri Karti, but it was too late. She takes the secret to her grave. Or does she? Next scene as Hermann's polishing his musket in the barracks, the spooky old Countess appears to him as a ghost, wheeled on by a splendid piece of stage machinery amidst a flurry of stage smoke, and reveals the three cards to him: the Three, the Seven and the Ace of Spades. This was one of the better scenes in the whole show. Before this there had been a lot of merely musical scenes (as Patak referred to them) with no action and hardly any stage business. Once the stage smoke was billowing Patak knew that things were hotting up. And besides, Patak knew from previous trips to the Smetana Theatre that ghosts tended to be good value.

Then Hermann goes off to jilt his girlfriend, worthy Lisa, who promptly chucks herself in the river. Another grand scene with the swirling snow on the bridge in the moonlight.

The irony, of course, wasn't lost on Patak. Here was a character renouncing the limitations of the mundane domestic life for the pursuit of his vocation. He glanced across at Julia and wondered if she, like the family-sized soprano, sensed the axe that was about to fall on her.

At this stage Patak had got the gist of the tale and he slipped out early to sink a couple of beers, leaving Julia to work the parallels out for herself. The only thing that puzzled him was why it was called The Queen of Spades. By rights, the opera should be called The Ace of Spades, as after all that was the card that was set to bring him riches.

Of course, Julia was pretty furious when she joined him in the Gropius restaurant when the curtain finally went down. That's it, she said. That's the last time I get you a ticket for the Smetana. I'll go with my mother again in future. Patak let her fume in peace for a moment. She'd clearly woken up to the parallels in the opera and felt the impending announcement. For Patak, it was just a question of deciding on the right moment to let fall the axe.

—The difficult thing is there's no one to talk to about this scheme. In fact, you are the first, discounting Julia, and she just can't seem to get it into her thick skull why this is such an exciting project…

—Julia?

—My ex.

Here was Patak in The Golden Stag going into details with Randy Hart, his new friend. Mala Strana people were different, friendlier, more open; it wasn't just sentimental claptrap.

—So when did you and her split up? asked Hart.

—Difficult to put a date on it. You know how it is. You wake up one morning and it's happened, it's split.

—The pod has split.

—Exactly.

Patak mused for a necessary moment.

—We're just different animals, he said. She likes opera and ballet; I like the circus.

—I see entirely, said Hart.

—Yes, all those pirouettes they just give me indigestion. Give me the bears and the cossacks any day.

—Indeed, acquiesced Hart: The bears and the cossacks; the noblest of circus numbers.

—The noblest, yes the noblest, the numéro de prestige I always call it. Have you ever noticed how all circuses always close with cossacks and bears? Ever notice that?

—Can't say that I have. Though now you come to mention it...

—Any circus worth its salt of course.

—No no, you're quite right, quite right. They always close the show with bears and cossacks.

Patak made a smug moue with his mouth.

—Fascinating, fascinating, said Hart, and then after clearing his throat: Still, now you're a free agent with you're ex-partner out of the way.

—Exactly. Exactly.

—And that liberates a creative mind I should think, concluded Hart.

Patak smacked his thigh:

—Exactly. Exactly. Exactement!

—Not that I'd know about creativity of that nature, admitted Hart. I am of a different breed. My instincts are commercial, and that's how I know you're onto a winner with your quiz show game show stuff. Everybody loves a game show.

—Especially one that deals in antagonisms, right?

—Yes. Especially. But any kind of a show.

—Yes but the point about mine is that it is different. Patak grinned. It is actually different. Antagonisms, he intoned.

—Right you are! chimed in Hart, looking back at him straight and dispassionate.

—Antagonisms, said Patak again, half to himself.

Hart turned his head away and gulped down three inches of beer.

Patak went on:

—When I think of all those years of slaving away in useless jobs, at the Insurance Times photo desk, checking on the right shade of rough red on some executive's blubbery cheek. And all the time I've been harbouring this idea, and you know what, Randy?

Randy Hart turned round to face Patak.

—I think it can work, I really think it can.

Patak laughed and Hart forced himself to join him. This was interminable drivel. What time was it?

—A little word in your ear, if I might, said Hart.

—Un petit mot, of course, go ahead.

—I've actually taken the liberty of inviting a friend of mine here this evening. She has some experience in these things. No, I haven't told her about your scheme, nothing, I thought you'd want to do that yourself, if and when you're ready. But it'll do no harm you meeting her.

Patak didn't know what to think.

—What, coming here to The Stag? A woman.

—A professional, corrected Hart.

Patak sunk his shoulders and slunk down onto the bar. If this was business talk it demanded conspiratorial posture.

—She knows her stuff, was Hart, lowering his voice: I don't know what I'd call her. An agent. An intermediary. An arranger. A money handler.

Each of these rejected epithets caused Patak to raise his eyebrows by a fraction.

—I'll slip away and leave you to it. I know you work best in the old one-to-one. Just sound her out and see what you think, but take it from me, she might just be the one who really gets this project off the ground.

—So you haven't mentioned the idea yet then?

—Not in so many words. Just one or two key elements to wet her lips.

—One or two key elements…

—Antagonisms, exclusion booths, pillories… A few key words to get her imagination working overtime. That's business!

—Of course of course. Clever.

—No, she knows you're an ideas man, but she doesn't know which one. I often introduce her to creative types like you. She normally slips me a few crowns for my troubles. It's hard for an uprooted guy like me to make a living without the proper papers, you'll appreciate that.

—Of course, of course, and don't think that you won't get ample appreciation from my purse for your efforts. You know you're the only one who really understands just how big this thing could get.

—Listening, counselling, interpreting, that's expert work, though not many people appreciate it.

Patak took his wallet out under the bar, came out with a few handsome notes and stuffed them into Hart's jacket pocket.

—Never let it be said that I don't act immediately on my word when called upon to do so, said Patak.

—Really there's no need for that, really, retorted Hart generously. I just thought we might institute a kind of commission basis, or, if you like a kind of weekly payment, maybe… four …thousand crowns.

—Why not, why not, pourquoi pas, why not indeed!

—Let me get this one! said Hart and a couple more splendid dark beers were forthcoming.

—Thank you, Mr Randy Hart. Thanks for everything.

They drank to that.

The beer was going down nicely. This was the way to do business. Informally, amongst people who understood each other, talked the same language. Patak knew he would never have such a good time with Julia, who didn't even like to drink for fear of spoiling her figure, which frankly had already seen better days. Patak mused on that sum that Hart had mentioned: a couple of thousand crowns a week or so, what was the figure he had agreed on? Four thousand. Fair enough! A man has got to live, and you had to give Hart his due, he'd been around when Patak had had to talk, he'd been the only one willing to listen, it was worth a salary in itself and four thousand crowns a week was only half what Patak picked up for his insurance paper work, hardly enough to live off in this day and age.

Patak felt a tap on his back.

—This is Lucretia, said Hart.

Patak turned and set eyes on what Hart had referred to as the agent. Patak put his beer down on the bar and wiped his moist hand on his jacket. They shook hands. A firm grip. Good in a negotiator. She was a nice looking filly too; good teeth, hair, strong limbed, good supple spine to her.

—Mr Patak, said Hart and stepped back to let the pair get acquainted.

—I've heard a lot about you Mr Patak, said the girl.

This came as something as a surprise.

—Antagonisms, said Patak and smiled broadly. Lucretia nodded and looked across to Randy Hart.

—I might just slip away for a packet of cigarettes, said Hart, and give you two the chance to get acquainted.

Lucretia was a tall brunette with a boy haircut, carefully trimmed and shaved along the neck and around the ears. She immediately threw off her heavy coat and folded it up on Hart's vacated bar stool. Beneath the coat she was wearing a green, square necked top and a pair of slacks. In the unlikely surroundings of The Golden Stag she looked over-glamorous. As Patak bought her a glass of port he saw her clipping on her ear-rings. So, she clips her battle gear on in full view. She means business, this one, thought Patak.

—Drink that down, he said.

She sipped and the dark red port overlaid her lips in a rather becoming way. As Patak launched into his presentation of antagonism theory he found his eyes resting mainly on those lips, now and again drifting up to the solid brown eye stare. It was a good presentation, he felt. It was the first fully implemented commercial account he had given—Julia and Hart had had different bits over a period of time. He had elaborated a medley of facial and hand gestures to go with the key words. This was a technique he had read up in a manual of advanced Western marketing strategies. For example, each time the word *antagonism* was mentioned he paused and lowered his head somewhat to be able to gaze up at Lucretia from beneath what the manual had called *bended brows*. Further techniques included the sudden up-beating at given points in the account—referred to in the manual as *pit stopping*—which is implemented by the introduction of simple linking phrases like *Now then* and *let's go further*. Child's play, actually. There was also the use of the index finger, which Patak deployed with the words *agonist, protagonist* and *antagonist*—in fact, anything with...gonist' in it, which made it easier to remember. Then there was what the manual called *punctuation policies*. This was the use of simple everyday gestures to create pregnant pauses in the text. The manual said you had to decide on one particular *punctuation act* at the beginning of your presentation and stick with it. The effect would then be like that of a recurring leitmotif in music. Ingenious. In this particular case the choice of *punctuation act* was clear-cut. Quite simply, Patak just took a sip of his beer. Of course, you had to vary the act. Sometimes eyes down towards the beer; sometimes the eyes still trained on the interlocutor;

sometimes the eyes closed in ostensible appreciation of the beer.

Mind you, he'd certainly had a few this evening. Lucretia was still on her first glass of port. Patak offered to get her another but she was happy just poking her raspberry lips at the rim of the glass.

—So what do you reckon? asked Patak when he'd completed his exposition.

That was the moment she chose for sinking the rest of her glass, tipping her head back to reveal a rather enticing gosier. It was an effective gesture, thought Patak. She had perhaps dipped into that manual herself.

She placed the empty glass down firmly on the bar.

—I think it's the best package I've heard of all year.

Package, no less. Wasn't such a bad little package herself.

—I think it's crying out to be given treatment. And I think we have to take it to Blackpool.

Blackpool. Now where had he heard that name before?

—That's where they're holding the European Game Show Salon this year in May. That's where all the deals are made. You can sell it to the British, the French, the Germans, the Italians; the big league. And once it's done by one of those, the Americans might take it up, and that's where the real money is.

She certainly seemed to know the ropes.

—Blackpool eh, said Patak. You really think I should take it to Blackpool.

—I'm convinced of it, she said.

—And where is Blackpool exactly?

—England. It's a beautiful resort on the North West Coast near Liverpool and Manchester.

—Liverpool and Manchester, mused Patak. Isn't that where the Beatles came from?

—Yes, and the cotton industry.

—Yes, of course, cotton, invaluable stuff.

—And Blackpool is close-by and home of the European entertainments industry. Have you never heard of the Tower of Blackpool?

Patak wracked his brain.

—Well, you've heard of the Tower of London. It's like that only in Blackpool, which has the added advantage of being near the famously pleasant Irish Sea.

—It sounds ravishing. Blackpool. It sounds like, I don't know, some kind of fairy tale land of clear waterstreams and aching seascapes.

—How poetic! said Lucretia. Well, there's no reason why one shouldn't combine pleasure with business, is there?

Patak laughed.

—If you want, you can leave it all to me, she said. I'll arrange the booking fee and all negotiations with the Blackpool authorities.

—Are you sure? This all sounds rather premature.

—Then there's the hotel. There's one hotel where you have to be. The Metropole hotel, very famous, lots of stars. A lot of the business is done in the hotel bar, you know, away from the Show itself. It's essential to reserve the rooms early. Ideally, we could get you a suite. The Victoria Suite is the famous one. Queen Victoria stayed there. It's still got all the items she used...

—Items?

—Oh, you know,... finger bowl... napkin... crown cushion where she placed her crown. Expensive, but it's worth it. It creates the right impression. It's unfortunate, but it's the way they are over there.

—Yes? Blackpool people?

—Blackpool people. You have to give the right impression, show them what league you're in. Superficial of course, but that's the West for you. And Blackpool people are notorious for it. We'll both go, of course, and perhaps I should get a room for Randy too.

—By all means, of course, Randy has to come. Where would I be without Randy?

—We'd better get it all sorted out as quickly as possible. Blackpool is only once a year. We don't want to miss it.

—Of course not.

She had taken a little pocket calculator out.

—You'll need to come up with… let me see… inscription fee, stand, installation fee… then there's the rooms…

—Suites, corrected Patak.

—Suites, yes, the suites… three suites…

—That's right. We must have a suite for Randy Hart as well.

—Make sure we get the Victoria Suite, said Patak.

—Oh, the Victoria Suite. Do you think so?

—If that's what it takes, said Patak.

—Fine.

Lucretia tapped in the extra figures. She went on:

—Then there's the air travel plus entertainment and drinks etc. plus sundries which is an extra 20%, you never know what might crop up in Blackpool.

—No, I imagine not.

—So we're talking about an initial outlay of around 200,000 Crowns, give or take the fluctuations in currency exchange rates. Let's call it 220,000.

Patak winced.

—Two hundred thousand Crowns!

—Say Two hundred and Twenty to be on the safe side.

Patak gulped.

—We're talking Blackpool. And Blackpool is… well… Blackpool.'

They laughed.

## Chapter Three: Mandryka

IT WAS about this time that Julia started to receive the attentions of a suitor by the name of Mandryka. Mandryka was an exuberant and unconventional figure, in this much the opposite of Patak who, it was now becoming clear to Julia, was—to put it bluntly—a bit of a square. With Mandryka at least there was a laugh. When they had met at the Smetana Opera House, where Julia was accompanying her aunt to a production of The Magic Flute, he had marched up and wooed her in the old lady's presence. He waited for her one Saturday afternoon—in fact it was the same afternoon on which Patak had seen his Sparta Prague radio commentary interrupted by Julia's nightie—and pounced on her at about six o'clock as she was coming up the steps of her apartment block. It was barefaced audacity to hunt her down like that, but at least it proved his enthusiasm and after a year of Patak's meagre sense of life, Julia approved. He had actually followed her to Patak's and waited outside the block in blustery rain before following her home. Of course he might have revealed himself at any moment but the shadowing amused him.

Mandryka was a forty-two-year-old powerhouse, both in physique and intellect who had started his career as an academic, specialising in the German Romantic period in music, literature and fable (as one of his lecture courses went) but who at the age of thirty-five had given up the way of the mind and gone into business, building up a chain of chocolate shops throughout the city using a horse and cart to deliver the chocolate from factory to distributors as the special marketing gimmick to seduce children. The sight of Mandryka's chocolates wending their way through the yards and allies of the old town, and the clop clop clop of Chocky the Horse echoing upon the quaintly preserved cobbles was a familiar Prague experience to any habitués of the old town.

With Mandryka life went with a bang. There were ideas—real ones, not inane quiz show nonsense. He had the knack of making things happen. With Patak progress of any sort was murky and labyrinthine. The day Mandryka followed Julia back to her apartment, after she had let him in for a visit of the square meterage and a view of the West looking vista—he had professed to being curious about the untergang at that particular end of town—they had shared a drink and made love. The drink was Whisky Moonshine, a concoction of his, and the love-making had followed before Julia could even tip her eager throat back to down the delicious sugary dregs. He pounced, and Julia fell back onto the rug and succumbed. *Do you submit?* he said. *I submit, I submit,* she said. He took her glass and downed it for her. *You're too slow,* he said. *Aren't you? Yes,* she said. *Yes. Do you submit?* he said. *Yes,* she said. *I submit, I submit. Say it again,* he said. *Say I submit to Mandryka.* And Julia said it. *Louder,* he said. *Say it louder. Say I submit to Mandryka.* And Julia said it again, louder. *I submit to Mandryka. I submit to Mandryka.*

That was the way of it with Mandryka. He was quick as the brown fox and unpredictable. That was what made him fun. Monday afternoon he was round at her place again. She recognised his silhouette at the frosted window. That's Mandryka's silhouette, she thought to herself, and paused a moment before opening the door. Looking at his Chinese shadow behind the frosted glass, Julia was struck by the somewhat monstrous protrusion of his chin. It stuck out like a knob on a door or a rounded flourish at the end of a bannister. It seemed solid and reassuring, as though made of wood or rosy apple. Mandryka knocked again and turned full on to the glass. Although Julia knew he couldn't see her, it was as if his eyes burnt straight through the opaque window. For an instant Julia toyed with the idea of not opening the door. It was, she knew, a decisive moment. She wanted to open the door. She wanted to see Mandryka, to have his full face encounter hers, to be with him. And yet, out of a kind of lethargy, she almost didn't. For she had arrived at a little moment of equilibrium, and she felt able to think; or rather to breathe right. The moment felt very good. It was not at all the business of betraying Patak. That didn't concern her, or at least was not a preoccupation of hers at that moment. It was a purely physical peace that she would have quite liked to retain. But she didn't. She started to feel an impatient tugging within her, and she breathed out and went to open the door for Mandryka.

Patak came away from his job with 8,800 Crowns a week, which meant that, counting on the basis of 52 weeks per annum, he could earn 457,600 Crowns a year. Now Lucretia was saying that it would cost him just about that much for the week's trip to Blackpool. Arithmetic was not Patak's greatest strength but whichever way he looked at it, things didn't add up. Naturally, he had savings. 900,000 Crowns all told, give or take a Crown or two. But he had vowed not to touch this nest egg, and if he did withdraw more than a fixed minimal amount per year—about 25,000—his interest rate would be cut from Gold to Silver.

Patak was musing on these things next day at work in the Insurance Age offices. The Insurance Age was one of a stable of newspapers and magazines dealing with the business world in Prague and the international community. Patak's job was officially the Picture Editor for the Insurance Age, but he also helped out on Haulage and Shipping as well as the Banking Bonus publications. A lot of the time there wasn't that much to do, so Patak had learnt to get his head down and pretend to be busy sifting through the photo library in a little office at the back of the main open plan area. The little office also contained the photocopy machine and the coffee machine, but Patak was the only one who took up residence there, so that it had become, so to speak, his own office.

Patak reported to the News Editor, Tycho Hedko, but in general Tycho had more pressing business to attend to and, even though he probably guessed that Patak was not doing anything constructive with the picture library, he let it go. Only once had he intercepted Patak in the Picture Library office and asked him if he was up to anything urgent or would he mind coming into the land of the living and sorting out a mug shot of the Prague Reinsurance Group chairman, which to Patak intimated that Tycho knew he wasn't doing anything important at the back of the photocopier.

Patak supposed that he'd have to forgo the Gold. He was thirty-eight. Fortune might not hold out her hand to him again, and in future years he would surely regret his lack of ambition if he now insisted on holding onto his paltry Gold interest rate. Why, Blackpool was all about real money, and, although the investment was hardly gilt-edged, it was at least one in which he could throw his entire creative self. Yes, Patak was convinced it was the right thing to do. It was the courageous thing. And anyway, he'd still have almost 700,000 Crowns in his account and the Silver Interest Rate wasn't that bad.

Patak went out of the office and crossed the floor of the main sub editing department. He walked past the Business Bonus subs, who would be working on page three—it was midday and pages three and four, nine and ten went off to the printers at two. The Business Bonus people tended to be older types who'd worked in the office for years. They gave Patak the creeps. He didn't want to be still in the job at their age. In fact, he didn't want to be in this job one second longer than he had to.

The Blackpool affair gave him a glimmer of hope. Sure, he was losing 400,000 Crowns of his hard-earned savings, but it was a kind of investment towards the future. What if he did sell the idea for his show to one of the big corporations, which seemed a distinct possibility now that he had Lucretia working on the job. That girl was dynamite. If the BBC bought the idea, he'd be rolling in it. And then, who knows, they might take him on as special consultant. What was he saying? He'd have stuff like that written into the contract. He'd insist on a credit. You know the type. Based on an idea by... And every time the show was repeated, or a spin-off was made from the original idea, he'd stand to make a mint. This was how Lucretia had explained it to him. With the initial outlay—financial and other—if you played your cards right, you were looking at a sure-fire winner. After all, there was nothing wrong with the idea. It was just the way it was sold. That's what had been holding him back all this time. And now he was addressing the issue.

Patak rapped on the glass door of the General Manager, Gary Vats.

—What is it, Patak?

—I wanted a word about the summer holidays.

Patak slipped into the office.

—Sit down, said Vats and opened his ledger. Vats nervously touched the pencil he always wore behind his ear.

—I should have ten days coming to me this summer and I'd like to put my bid in now for that last week of May.

—I thought you always took first week in July and went down to Pec to see your mother.

—More pressing business this year.

Vats looked up from behind the ledger to briefly inspect Patak.

—Well, he said, his nose down in the ledger again. It says here that Rodky's got the last week in May.

—What, already?

—Yes, he takes it every year. He goes to the May Fest in Vienna, I seem to remember. He's got a brother-in-law there.

—Well I have to have that week.

—You can't both have it. You know that. You'll have to have a word with him. But if he won't budge he was first.

Patak was silent. Rodkey was a difficult character. He worked mainly on the Haulage and Shipping mag and covered for Patak on Insurance Age when Patak was off. He was in fact the one person who had to be there if Patak was away hammering out big deals in Blackpool.

Patak went back into the main office and spied Rodkey across the News Agency Printer which was spilling out information, probably on the recent earthquake in Southern Africa—Patak already had a photo lined up for page one. Rodkey was a tricky adversary. He'd been in the job longer than Patak and knew the ins and outs of office manoeuvres. He was a beefy forty-year-old who liked to roll his sleeves up and make huge swaying motions of his shoulders and torso when he worked. He thought Picture Editor was a manual job, and seemed through his body language to hark back to a time when the production of pictures had been a more physical process. It was as if he were extracting prints from out of his computer with gusty heaves, which of course was not necessary, you just pressed a few keys on the computer and fooled around with the colours and the size. All this meant that he tended to interpret mere verbal approach of any sort as treachery.

Rodkey looked across to Patak. Patak prepared his friendliest, most alluring of smiles. At that moment he saw himself through Rodkey's eyes: younger, more elegant, suaver.

—Tricky bastard! said Rodkey.

Patak was slightly taken aback. Rodkey was looking over a photograph. This machine's playing up again, Patak. It keeps tricking me into over-doing the colour.

—Ah! said Patak and strolled over. He looked down at the picture. A jeep was sinking into mud in an African village. Floods had devastated swathes of Western Africa.

Julia was going to be disappointed. He hated letting her down. Patak was on his way round to her apartment near the Brevnov Monastery. She lived in a modern block that looked out onto a park, sharing the apartment with her dog, an ugly mongrel with a swaggering limp of a gait. Patak was going round for tea. Julia always had to have a formal pretext for any social intercourse, as if the reason for coming round was first and foremost to partake of tea or elevenses and then incidentally to see her. The ideal situation for her would be to share a pot of tea and two Prague gingers and eliminate all conversation. For just once in her life Patak would have liked to oblige her; before he left her definitively. Of course, when Julia was on alien territory it was another story. Then all was chaos. Like her coming round on Saturdays at ten to three. In Patak's apartment she seemed to delight in upturning his well worked routines with the most anarchic of pretexts. Nighties to be tried on; exercise videos to be tried out absolutely that very instant; she sometimes even brought that limping mongrel along with her.

Patak had taken special pains to kit himself out in his most alluring fashion: his splendidly tailored pale green linen suit with a Bohemia green bow-tie on the backdrop of a crisp white shirt. He was the picture of clean-cut efficiency.

When Patak buzzed on the entry phone Julia let him straight in without a word, which was unusual. She who was so careful about who gained access to the block and who had campaigned for the residents to pay an extra fee to hire a doorman to be on the door at all times of day or night. She must have caught a glimpse of him out of the window.

When Patak got in the apartment, music was going full pelt.

—Turn it down, he roared.

Julia emerged from the bedroom. She was wearing a trouser suit that Patak had never seen before.

—Oh it's you, she said and went across to turn the disc off.

—Of course it's me. Who else could it be? You don't have to turn it off. Just down.

—No, that's all right.

—What on earth is it? It's not more of that ballet music, is it?

—No it's Bruckner.

—Since when did you like that stuff?

—Oh, I've been getting to like it for a time now.

—It's depressing.

—Oh, I don't think so. It fires me up.

She was standing with her hands on her hips and her legs apart like a regular Walkyrie.

—And where did you get that trouser suit from?

—I didn't get it. It was a present.

Patak had no patience with her when she was in a mood like this.

—Never mind, never mind, he said impatiently, waving his hand in the air. Forget I ever even asked.

At the back of his mind Patak wondered whether he had already seen the trousers suit or not. He knew he hadn't bought it for her. He would never buy such a thing. But maybe she'd shown it him one time. She bought herself such a lot of stuff. How could he be expected to remember it all?

—You're all togged up, she said.

—Well, that's what I'm here about. About tonight. I have to go out for a meeting about the Antagonism show, so I shaln't be coming round.

—I didn't know you were going to.

—No, well, I thought maybe you thought I might. You know like when I pop round now and again. Well, tonight I can't. So don't go expecting me.

—All right then, she said, plain as you like. What was up with her today?

—Yes, I'm talking antagonisms tonight. Talking business. This thing is actually starting to... you won't believe me of course... but it really is actually starting to get off the ground one way or another. I mean, if I were selling shares in it, which I'm not, don't get me wrong, because I wouldn't sell them anyway, but I mean if I were selling shares in it, this would be the time that the share price tripled or something.

—So, you're making money on it, are you?

Patak pursed his lips as though he were weighing up whether or not to reveal the full extent of his windfall.

—Let's just say nothing's certain for the moment.

Then Patak laughed. He let out a buoyant, youthful, revelatory laughter, that was not meant to be observed coldly. It was meant to be shared by another drunken participant in his excitement. Julia, however, just watched him. She was pleased to see a kind of youth, albeit complex ridden and corseted, swimming up from behind his eyes in his ugly abandon, and she felt on reflection that, yes, she approved, he was following his heart, however wayward it was, good luck to him, but, she knew—it seemed to come home to her at that moment too—that she did not love him and actually never had. Why she had let his absurd mouth slaver at her and his ordinary, ordinary self contemplate a kind of yoking up with her as a twin team of oxen, she did not understand. He really was such a buffoon. How she had put up with his presence next to her at Swan Lake before Christmas was a mystery. The only moments in the entire ballet that seemed to produce a flickering of appreciation from him were the tableau at the end of scenes where the prima donna would be hoisted into the air by two of the main ballet dancers. These moments—or rather anything that involved hoisting and yanking—produced roars of approval and bursts of applause from him, whereas the rest, the whole spectacle of sublime grace and poise gave rise to nothing more than an indifferent yawn.

Patak stopped laughing. He was scratching his face and blowing.

—You look happy, she said.

Patak steadied his breathing. He pulled a face.

—Happy, happy. What do we mean by happy? If we mean that I'm convinced that the antagonism project is finally starting to beat its wings and take off, then yes, I am.

—Well, I'm pleased for you.

Patak was taken aback by her grace in the matter. From the very beginning it was as if she had been willing the project to come to nothing. If it took off, if it sailed, it would be despite her. And yet now here she was as bold as brass saying she wished him well.

The entry phone rang.

Julia opened the door downstairs without a moment's hesitation. But it could be anybody. A murderer; a rapist; a door-to-door salesman; a religious believer. Anybody. What had come over her?

—That'll be Mandryka, she said.

Patak was observing her now. He hardly heard what she said.

They waited. Patak was thinking: what are we waiting for? But he knew it was something.

A rat-a-tat-tat came on the door. Julia slipped away from where she had been standing at his side. They had been standing side by side like an Adam-and-Eve in a medieval tapestry, as though revealing themselves to a hidden audience, unconcerned with relating to each other, just fulfilling the ineluctable process of fate, that they sin and be sent into the world. In the same way, Patak felt at that split second to be no more than a marionette in the hands of another.

The door swung back and there was an ugly, large headed individual with the dog in his arms.

—He wouldn't go in the lift, so I had to carry him, said the man.

He looked at Patak. He walked into the apartment. Patak wasn't sure what was going on. The stranger put the dog down. Patak looked across the room to Julia. Roderigo walked off into the kitchen.

—Patak, this is Mandryka, said Julia.

The man held out his hand. Patak shook it.

—Charmed, said the man.

Patak said nothing. He looked at the stranger suspiciously. The man went into the drawing room and sat down on a hard-backed chair.

—Come and have a drink, said Julia and followed the man into the room but she was speaking to Patak.

—Sherry for everyone, she said.

She took the bottle out of the sideboard and rounded up three glasses.

—Good idea, said the man.

The stranger was looking very pleased with himself. Patak walked unsteadily across the room and sat down in his armchair. Normally Julia sat opposite in the other armchair and they swapped anecdotes over tea. Now Julia was placing herself at the table with the stranger. Politesse, no doubt. As was the sherry she was now handing round.

—I advised Julia to get some sherry in, started the stranger. It's the perfect early evening drink. I picked the habit up from a couple of British colleagues of mine at the university. Not that it's a British drink, of course, but they seem to have embraced it most wholeheartedly. It's a warming drink, don't you think? I was saying to Julia. I'll buy a joint and cook up a leg of lamb or a side of pig or something, and deck it out with turnips and carrots and swede, and bring along some *fine wines and choice cheeses*—here the stranger put on a voice—with some chocolates and brandy to round it off. What do you say? Are you game for that?

Patak could hardly believe he was addressing him.

—No. Patak's busy tonight, intercepted Julia.

—Shame about that, said the stranger. It'll have to be another time then. I have some top wines, as I say, and this is the season to warm up with them. Excuse me for boasting but it's as well you know so that we can fix a firm date for it.

Patak nodded and muttered.

—Next week then, said the man. Any day. I have nothing on and Julia will let me know when it suits you best.

—Thursdays are good, aren't they, Patak, said Julia.

Patak cleared his throat.

—I don't know about Thursdays, he said.

—You always say it's the best night of the week for an outing, said Julia.

—Certain kinds of outing, said Patak.

—All you have to do is get yourself round here and eat and drink your fill. Conversation we can do without, if that's what's bothering you.

Patak took a gulp of his sherry.

—No, said Julia. Patak loves to talk. I sometimes can't get a word in when he's on his pet subject.

—Julia did mention your ambitions in the world of family entertainment, said the stranger. But do be careful in that business. Don't risk anything till there's a signature on the dotted line. Sharks abound, Mr Patak.

This was getting beyond a joke. Not only was this total stranger lecturing him on his own field but Julia—in what was surely some pathetic attempt at a practical joke—was egging him on. She had probably hired this grotesque from the back pages of one of those women's magazines she was forever flipping through. But joke or no joke, Patak disapproved of her revealing any information at all about what was a project that had to stay under lock and key. The grotesque—my god, was he ugly!—was still rabbeting on.

—Friends of mine have lost bagsful, especially with foreigners. Beware, Mr Patak, beware the slippery tongues of the show business breed. We Czechs are naives in the business world. Watch out for Western wiles. Believing that success is granted to the individual who strives against the odds and triumphs is one of the most insidious lies the West is foisting on us. All is not possible, Mr Patak. American dreams may fool Americans. But we Czechs have been raised in a more realistic school. Remember that.

Patak put his sherry down on the carpet.

—Sir, he said. I don't know in what magazine Julia found you and I dare say you're only doing your job here tonight and I should really be addressing myself to Julia, but I'll address myself to both of you in saying that this practical joke has gone far enough. I don't know whether Julia has paid you your cheque or not, but I strongly suggest you finish your sherry and get off back to your kind, be they balloon benders or horoscope readers. Julia has, perhaps naively, revealed information to you that she should never have let out of the Pandora's box, but I am fortunate in knowing that although you clearly have a passing acquaintance with what you stupidly refer to as the world of family entertainment, your knowledge can be no more than cursory. You have probably never even heard of the Blackpool Salon of Quiz Games or a host of such-like institutions I could cite to you if I had the time and inclination, neither of which as a busy man I at present have. And so, sir, I bid you good day. And as for you, Julia, my pressing engagement prevents me from adequately relaying the extent of my disappointment in your misapprehension of our state of semi-cohabition and confidence, a state I can only exhort you to think on over the next few days.

So saying, Patak heaved himself up from the armchair and stormed out to a storm of laughter from the stranger. Patak slammed the door on the splutterings of the grotesque threepenny performer.

Patak was first in the vodka and herring bar where he had arranged to meet with Lucretia. He had booked the back table to be sure to be away from the mass that crowded at the top end around the ballad singer who plied his trade on Thursdays, Fridays and weekends. The rough tones of the songster would drift to the back of the room and be heard as just a nudging reminder of the popular world and its cabals and intrigues. There was even a curtain you could ask to be drawn around the table if needs be, though there was an extra fee for the use of this feature.

Patak installed himself with his back to the wall, so that he could see Lucretia when she came in, and ordered a bottle of Regular Pure 60%. The waiter set the bottle down on the table top and placed the a couple of squat pony glasses down by it.

As Patak eyed the frosted glass of the vodka bottle, he ran his mind along a channel that opened up. He had to get that week free for Blackpool. The only way was to persuade Rodkey to take another week, and that might have to be through a cash inducement of one sort or another. Rodkey wasn't above the charms of the financial arrangement. It had happened before. Three or four years ago Rodkey had persuaded Patak into agreeing to a modification in their job description due to computerisation only with a large cash bonus. The new equipment had actually made both their jobs easier, but Rodkey had stuck it out in the face of Patak, who feared management retribution, and the editor to earn them their premium. Patak should have been grateful to him for getting them a few extra thousand Crowns, but he felt only a nagging unease that Rodkey had revealed him to be bit of a coward, and the incident had only fuelled Rodkey's distrust of Patak's treacherous ways.

Patak had just decided to invite Rodkey to dinner when Lucretia arrived.

—I see you've got the best table in the house, she said as she pulled her chair round from face-on to side-by-side.

She sat down alongside Patak and then turned her head to smile at him.

—Won't we be better opposite each other? he said. That way we won't have to strain.

—There'll be no straining, she said. I thought we might need to go over a few documents together.

—Of course, of course, said Patak. The ways of the financial world are sometimes opaque to me, I must admit.

—Artists, grinned Lucretia and as though acting on a prompt from him, she nudged up closer so that their two chairs touched. She was next to him in a kind of sisterly way.

Patak reached across to pour the vodka into her glass, but she was so close that his elbow scooped lightly across her rib cage.

—Oops, he said.

His unsteady hand poured out two poneys for them and he pushed the bowl of fish across the table towards her.

—Herring? he said.

She had taken out some papers from her shoulder bag and was spreading them out across the table. Then she laid out a blank sheet of paper on top of them and got out a red pen. On the paper she started to draw some ovals; in the middle of the paper one oval, then up above it three more ovals. Then underneath the central oval she drew a cross.

—Ingenious, said Patak.

As she was at work, Patak imbibed the odours. The odourless vodka first of all, the herring and vinegar, and also mixing in the magma of perfume, moisturiser and shampoo that overlaid her own personal scents. She was dressed in a kind of splendid purple jump suit, but tightly fit and short sleeved. She inspired massive confidence. She had no acne of any sort. It was skin that could not produce blockages. The efficient high quality stuff you saw in glossy magazines. As she shifted her biro on the sheet her chair clacked a little against his.

The ballad songster was coming out to a ripple of applause. The evening was wearing on now. The misunderstanding or whatever it had been with Julia was left behind in the afternoon slot, he was moving on now to evening entertainment. The ballad singer was starting up with 'The Bride of Odnovsky Town'.

*The sun is shining in the trees*
*The starlings singing free,*
*It takes me back to Odnovsky*
*And what she meant to me...*

—This is you, said Lucretia.

Patak focused back on the paper, where she was writing his name next to the cross on the lower half of the page.

—Or rather X plus C. Patak plus concept.

—We could call it X plus A for Antagonism, he chipped in, before correcting himself. No no, you're absolutely right. Let's stick with C for concept, otherwise we'd have to have P for Patak instead of X.

—We'll stay with X plus C, shall we?

—As you were, as you were, said Patak jovially.

Lucretia moved her pen up to the three upper ovals.

—These are Europe, the US and the Rest of the World.

—Very good, very good, said Patak and rubbed his hands together. This was great fun.

The songster had finished the tragic tale of the bride of Odnovsky Town, drowning her in the town well as always and had now moved onto telling a few jokes.

—*My horse has ten legs. Two fore legs and two hind legs. Two fores are eight plus two hind, that makes ten legs. Therefore has my horse ten legs.*

Patak couldn't help laughing. It was a silly joke, but very clever when you thought about it... He looked across to see if Lucretia was laughing with him, but her eyes were down on the sheet.

Lucretia had moved her pen down to the central oval and was tapping it.

—Access to those markets, those production companies, those television stations for Patak and concept comes through here. What is the channel, Patak?

He knew the answer. Of course he knew the answer. He had heard it so many times in recent weeks so that its spondaic tread was a now dear familiar paw mark on the snowscape of his imagination. He spoke it before she could put pen to paper. The answer was Blackpool. What else? What else?

After she had neatly written the word in the oval, Patak asked for the curtains to be drawn. He got up and poured two more ponys for them and they started looking at her break-down of the figures for the Blackpool trip. It actually came to slightly more than what she had said last time, but it was good to see the whole enterprise taking concrete shape before his eyes.

—The way I see the week is this, she said. We arrive on the Friday before the event to give us a couple of days to get used to the set-up. In this business it's important to be at your ease. It all works so much on feeling.

—Of course, said Patak.

Lucretia looked at him. As they were sitting together to look at the figures her face was up close to his. It was actually a rather round face, Patak realised, very slav-looking with narrow eyes and a rather flat, sheer nose, ideally suited for placing behind a vizard of some kind.

—Like us, she said. That's how we work together. It functions on feeling. We trust each other, and what's it based on? Intuition. Feeling.

Patak nodded and lowered his gaze demurely. Lucretia looked at his sorry scalp line. His hair was thinning and she could not see whether what lay beneath the sparse outcrop was scalp or forehead skin; his forehead was creeping higher. His modesty made him like a young girl; he was ridiculous.

She went on:

—So that first weekend we scout round and build up the contacts. As I've already said, most of the work is done in the restaurants and night-clubs outside of the usual exhibition hall. A chance meeting in a typical English pub could lead to that all important deal.

He thrilled at the idea. He had never been a great traveller. He usually spent his summer holidays with his mother in Pec and had once been to Munich in Germany. But he had never ventured beyond there and his knowledge of England was limited to what he had seen on police series of the sixties and seventies mostly starring Roger Moore. The idea of striking deals in a genuine English pub sent shivers of anticipation down his spine. As far as he could make out, Blackpool was the playground of the Londoners. The rich and famous would dash up there from the capital at weekends to meet their own in the celebrated surroundings in the shadow of the much vaunted tower.

Although Patak had always ignored the temptation to travel and had preferred instead to acquire a nest egg of savings—which was now proving invaluable, incidentally—he had always known, deep within himself, that the day would come when he'd be hatching deals in some high-class English public house in Saint Tropez or Blackpool.

—Monday the exhibition proper starts. By Friday we'll be looking for a signature or two on the dotted line. The ideal would be to auction the big dealers off one against the other...

What's more, he thought, I'll be there in style. Sipping English sherry in my panelled Hotel Blackpool suite with my agent. What was the name of that special suite she had mentioned? The Victoria Suite, was it? Who knows what the outcome might be? Lucretia was a good-looking woman, and she and Randy Hart were clearly old friends with no romantic inclinations of any sort towards each other. The girl must be seeing something in him for her to be investing all this time in the project. Who knows—and inwardly Patak's eyes twinkled here—maybe it wasn't just professional.

It was as if Patak were waking up into a marvellous new world, the exciting world of the Mala Strana perhaps, or else emerging from the chrysalis he had been living in up till now. Later that night in bed with the occasional night revelry audible on the Lenski Avenue below, Patak thrilled. The key to the the door that was his bed had turned and let him silently through into another place.

## Chapter Four: Randy and Lucky

RANDY HART and Lucretia Tourishova shared a one room flat in the heart of the old town. They had met in the Narodni Fast Club on Narodni Way a couple of weeks after Hart had settled on the East Bank. Lucretia, or Lucky as she liked to call herself, had migrated to the East Bank like Hart a couple of years previously, so they recognised themselves as comrades-in-arms right from the start.

Neither had the right papers to work in the Old Town. Hart was flat broke. Lucky managed to make a few Crowns a week from a couple of appointments with gentlemen of means that she had managed to institutionalise. One of the gentlemen of means she had managed to institutionalise lent her the studio apartment which he had bought as an investment for his kids. While he waited for the housing market to take off, it came in handy for his little rendez-vous away from the wife. The problem for Hart was that this guy—a Mr Waldner—had his own key to the place and was liable to pop round at any moment. Still, it was an inconvenience worth accepting for the advantage of living for free. Moreover, Waldner also kept the fridge nicely stocked.

The Patak business was just one of many that Hart and Lucky were juggling with whilst looking for more gainful occupation. Lucky had heard about the Blackpool Salon from one of her clients, and the fellow Patak seemed like a tragic enough gull to fall for it. They would keep it up for as long as they could and disappear only when it was no longer possible to continue with the pretence. Whether that would be before the Blackpool Salon—which would mean merely making off with the cash for the suites and the flights—or whether they could find a way of actually going to Blackpool and prolonging the scam beyond the ten-day holiday they had not yet decided. Hart was all for taking the trip money and as much as possible up until the fateful week and then making off into the night, but Lucky was confident of her hold over Patak and felt it might be worth going through with the Blackpool thing and chancing her arm into the après-Blackpool.

These were questions the two of them were musing over one sunny afternoon. The sun was streaming in through the sixth floor window. Waldner had left on a business trip. He was away for five days at least, probably even longer, as he would have to go back and placate the wife for a few days on his return.

Lucky was moaning about Patak:

—I mean, this money's just daily bread. There's no colour to it. It's just daily allowance for life. We need a decent block. When are you seeing him next?

—We're going to see the Sparta Prague—Star Prague derby tonight. I'll see about more bread then.

Hart lay back on the bed and blew out smoke from his cigarette. He had recently been able to upgrade his brand of cigarettes to Park Lane, the more sophisticated smoke, if one could believe the adverts. At least it was better than the filthy Mala Strana brands he'd been used to. He hoped he'd never have to touch a Kepler ever again.

Lucky was over at her dressing table making up her face. She was applying some new lipstick she'd picked up from Kotva—Glamour Rouge.

Mind you, it was no good complaining and (to be honest) they could hardly have worked it better than they were doing. She had even managed to up the allowance she was getting from Patak last time they'd met, although the time was coming when she would have to produce the booklet on Antagonism that she was forever promising. Of course, to do that she would have to read all the trash that Patak had churned out of his PC, as well as reproduce the cash she had just splashed out on beauty products, which was of course impossible. Unless she hit the jackpot on the lottery, which (to be fair) was at least ten times as likely now that she had started buying ten instead of a mere one ticket a week.

—What do you think? she asked and turned to face Hart with glamour rouge daubed over her lips.

—Fancy spancy, said Hart.

—Pretty ace, eh?

—Smart tart.

Lucky went back to work on her face.

Hart pushed himself up from the bed and went over to the fridge. Lucky usually got Waldner to stock up properly before a trip, though he did insist on shopping with Lucky and so there was a limit to the number of beers she could reasonably request. Still, there were a few at the back there. Hart reached in and pulled one free from the grouping.

—Beer?

Lucky mumbled a *no*. She had her mouth freshener in and was swilling.

After a moment she went over to the sink and spat.

—You should try this now and then, she said

Hart just looked at her.

—It'd make a change from smelling of beer all the time. It's not snogworthy, you know, whatever you think.

—And do you think all that peppermint mouthwash is such a snogworthy deal for me.

—At least it's hygienic.

Lucky turned back to the mirror and made eyes at herself:

—And there's the cigarettes. Those Kepler's taste foul.

—That shows how much you know. I switched to Park Lanes two weeks ago.

—Excuse me for not knowing the difference between one filthy smoke breath and another. Yellow teeth is yellow teeth.

—Well, I'm no male model, if that's what you mean.

Hart puffed up his chest proudly. Lucky gargled.

—Classic! said Hart and laughed to himself.

After a moment he put his finger in his ear and twisted it round vigourously. When he brought out the wax he transferred it carefully from under his finger nail to the inside of his pocket. Snot and wax and any other discardia tended to harden nicely out of sight on the inside of the pocket and could then be chipped off and flicked out of sight.

—And what about Patak? he asked over the gargling.

Lucky spat and pulled a face:

—What about him?

—He's never tried anything on with you, has he?

Lucky shook her head, still pulling that face. The idea of Patak putting on the charm was a curious challenge to the powers of the imagination.

—If he did, came Hart following his train of thought, then it mightn't be such a bad idea.

—I like the way I get all the nice jobs, said Lucky.

—I'm not saying you have to, but don't go slamming him out, will you?

Lucretia arched her brows:

—Actually, he has invited me out.

—Oh yeah, where to?

—The circus.

—Oh he's not fed you all his rubbish about cossacks and bears, has he?

Lucky nodded and smiled sadly to recall the conversation:

—He does go on sometimes. Anyway, let's just hope it doesn't go any further than cossacks and bears.

—That's right. Let's hope he keeps his hands off your bear skin. Gettit? Let's hope he keeps his hand out of the honey jar,eh?...

—All right, all right, give it a rest...

—Classico! said Hart.

Hart guffawed to himself and scratched at his privates.

—Where are you off tonight anyway? he asked after a moment. The main thing for him was to keep abreast. That was the way he saw his contribution; keeping his ears pricked for any opening that might come their way.

—With a client.

—Who's that?

—Radost.

—And what are you doing?

—We're going out to see some show.

Hart nodded and pursed his lips together. In general, he approved of Lucky sharing herself out with the three regulars, Waldner, Radost and the new one whatever his name was. But now and again there were moments of pique, mostly at times when he had nothing much to do himself. Tonight, of course, it was all right. Patak had got tickets for the Sparta Prague–Star Prague match.

Hart pushed himself up from the bed and went over to the dressing table. He stood behind Lucky's chair and looked down at her.

—And what happens after the concert or whatever it is?

Lucky looked at him through the mirror.

—We come back here as usual, I suppose. Who knows? I told you what happened last time?

—About the costumes.

—Yes. Now we're getting there with the Thirty Years War costumes.

—That puts the tariffs up, I hope.

—Yes. It puts the tariffs up, she answered and gave Hart an unsympathetic look through the mirror. Still, it doesn't pay as much as psychoanalysts. Maybe I should set up shop as one of those.

Lucky specialised in role-plays. It was amazing what some of the East Bankers wanted to get up to.

Hart looked down at her uncertainly.

—I'd stick to what you're doing and just build up your clientele, he said.

—Oh yeah, and what are you supposed to be? My manager?

—That's right. Maybe you should pay me 20%.

—You already get at least 20% by living here for free. But the moment I get sick of it, then…

Here Lucretia made a flute-like whistling sound to imitate the sound of her skedadelling bag and baggage like some speedy cartoon character.

—Seems a shame, said Hart. It can't be that hard making a living out of dressing up as characters from the Thirty Years War and pretending to push an old guy out the window for cash.

For a moment Lucky said nothing. Then, as an afterthought:

—Who says he's an old guy?

—Classico! said Hart, smirking, then reached for his packet of Park Lanes.

When Patak met up with Hart in the Slavia Bar on the edge of Narodni Avenue opposite the National Theatre to take the tram out to the Sparta Prague ground, a sliver of doubt rose up within him like an unpleasant heartburn. This in no way resembled the homely afternoons spent by his radio set. It was an evening kick-off. The lights were appearing in windows along the river and casting shimmering light onto the water. Groups of supporters were gathering at the tram stop for the special match day trams to take them out to the stadium beyond the ring road. The groups of men stood uneasily on the street corner as if soliciting for work. They packed together in tight circles obeying some internal rules of group mechanics, eddying slightly and remaining sharply defined despite the sense of violent shifting from within.

Everyone was smoking. Hart too began to smoke. Patak saw his face illuminated by the match as he lit up in the twilight air. It was a large wide alien face and Hart was, now Patak came to think, a Mala Stranite. In the sudden illumination, which was like the sharp almost sacred focus of a seventeenth century Italian religious painting, you noticed the single strands of hairs that made up the eyebrows, the hugeness of the grain of the tear duct, the rawness of the skin on the inner nostril, the mechanics of the construction of that face. Patak also noticed how dirty Hart's fingernails were. It was a small and unimportant detail, he knew, but the sight of them in the harsh strip lighting of the bar was another jolt to his system.

The red tram arrived, fizzing sparks from the overhead wires in the now fallen night. They trailed on and sat with the men. Hart sat slightly turned away from Patak, his cigarette trailing blue smoke up into the confines of the bus. Hart was like a stranger. He seemed to belong to the mass of strangers here, the block of them constituting one monolithic edifice from which Patak was excluded.

As home supporters, Patak and Hart were making their own way to the ground. Whereas the away supporters of Star Prague would be hoarded in buses from the West Bank, then escorted by the police into the stadium and at the end of the match led back to the bus and ferried back to the Mala Strana. There would be no risk of rival fans meeting. The Star Prague fans were compartmentalised and separated by thirty metres of heavily policed terraces.

Inside the ground, into which they streamed with the Sparta fans as in one body, Patak was struck by the difference in the texture of the sound emitted by the crowd. On the radio the roar was a supple concentrated beast, efficient and hard edged. Here it was a vast implacable creature beating its awful wings. Its location was uncertain but it had eyes in all places.

Across the angle of the corner flag from where Patak was seated level with the edge of the penalty area were the massed ranks of the Star supporters at the Castle End of the ground. The were layered up one behind the other like an army of seething insect life. Brutality was built within them like some time bomb that might explode at any moment without instigation of any sort. Patak looked across to try and gauge the looks in those eyes but they were just too far off for him to decipher. They emitted a kind of sub-buzz within the general din and were all wearing the same kind of jerkin.

The players came out and the match got underway with very little fuss. Patak found it difficult to concentrate. The immediacy of the crowd about him was so much more engaging than the players running round on the pitch. He realised how much he needed the approval of a radio commentator to make sense of the game. Viewed from the terraces—about twelve steps up from pitch level—it was difficult to judge what was going on. His appreciation of the danger or thrill of the action followed the aggregated reaction of the crowd rather than his own spontaneous appreciation of the game. The whole thing was random: a ceaseless tangling of legs; constant chases for possession and then space; an interminable kickaround resembling an outsized prologue rather than the shapeliness of a match.

It was almost half time before Patak settled down to accommodate himself with the nature of the tussle. By his side Randy Hart—an avid Star supporter, although where they were seated with the Sparta Prague fans this had to be disguised—was producing an endless stream of moans, sighs and yelps, which he tried to caste in ambiguous morse.

Half-time was the business of queuing for beer and producing narrative out of the flurries of the first forty-five minutes. Hart said it was a good match and Star had come close on a number of occasions. There was one incident where Janek had been right through and brought a reflex save from the Sparta keeper, which must have been one of the saves of the season, he said.

—But did you see how he got down to it because Janek had met the shot just right and he's no fool in front of goal? said Hart.

—Yes, it was a great save all right, said Patak, but he wasn't really sure about the incident Hart was referring to.

—If we keep applying the pressure, Sparta'll have to crack, went on Hart, lowering his voice but needing to use the first person plural to identify with the Star Prague outfit.

Patak nodded. That was the way it worked; he knew from radio commentaries.

—No mercy, said Hart, his blood roused. No mercy, no mercy.

Patak smiled and looked at him for the second or third time that night with an indifference that he would rather not have felt.

They took up their places for the second half. They had managed to find a place higher up the terraces. Sparta continued their pressing game, forcing Star into mistakes without ever really threatening the Star goal. A few minutes into the half Hart cleared his throat.

—About the Blackpool trip, Hart started up as Nemecec the Star Prague wing back was moving forward from the back trying to beat the Sparta offside trap. I need to get some work done on your computer myself.

—Well, what's your computer?

—No, I don't think we're compatible. I need to work directly on the master machine, said Hart. It'll give me a chance to have another look at your latest notes on Antagonisms. You know, the creative mind does fascinate me.

Patak was infused by a warm glow.

—Well, I'll let you have the spare set of keys and you can let yourself in while I'm at work next week.

Nemecec had broken the offside trap and was bursting through on the goal.

—Fine, said Hart. It won't take long. I just need to run over a few things from the commercial point of view.

—Come round tomorrow night and I'll show you the files and have the spare keys ready for you.

Nemecec had struck. The ball sat nestling in the corner of the goal. The Star Prague fans went wild in their enclosure and Randy Hart, knowing that revelation at this stage would be fatal, did his best to contain his joy.

By this time Lucretia was slinked across the bed, counting well earned bank notes out slowly on the counterpane and smirking to herself. Her appointment had gone well. Radost had taken her out to what was called a Mozart banquet, a feast with musical accompaniment, all in period dress. All of which whet Radost's appetite for his own bout of fancy dress back at the apartment. Buoyed up by the wine, Radost had gone through his own scenario with rare flourish. The dressing up, the enactment of the Thirty Years War scenario, the sudden transition towards wordless sex had all ran its course smoothly and painlessly, as far as Lucretia was concerned. Now she was ten thousand Crowns better off.

The counterpane she was now stretched out on depicted the famous scene of defenestration which lay at the root of the Thirty Years War. In a tumble of scarlets and Prussian blues, three Catholic noblemen, Count

Martinic, Governor Slavata and Philip Fabricius are slung out of the window of the Court Chancellery in Hradcany Castle. Lucretia laid the one hundred Crown notes out onto Count Martinic's pink face and pushed the rest of the notes across the counterpane towards the stitching of the window through which appeared the roughly woven rooves of the old town.

She laid the counterpane out specially to receive Radost and complement the costumes he liked them both to wear. Today he had even brought a new jerkin and a large feather for the broad brimmed cap he insisted on sporting. Lucretia restricted herself to some cross-gartered slippers and a fully brocaded, heavily ribbed ball gown. It wasn't clear whether the style was quite contemporary to the events of 23rd May 1618, but Radost approved of it.

—I've picked up something special for this week. It's a new jerkin, Radost had said: Green... with fur about the collar.

—Very fetching, said Lucky, as he produced it from his carrier bag and held it against him. It was thigh length.

—I thought I'd wear it over the shirt.

—The one with claret ruffles.

—Yes and with the rope belt around the waist, and then with the hose and foot-wear.

—The suede ankle boots.

—Yes yes, and with the chain about the neck, the chain of state, and maybe the ruffly hat.

—Yes, I think that might well do the job.

Radost nodded, happy to have her approval:

—You do think that, don't you?'

—Yes, I do. You know I wouldn't say so if I didn't, don't you?

—Yes, said Radost. I know that.

Lucretia popped some gum into her mouth and started on a pile of five hundreds. The scene of defenestration being the main act of historical import from Bohemian history, the five hundred note illustrated exactly the same celebrated defenestration as the counterpane, but a few seconds before, when the Protestant supporters of Count Thurn were rushing into the room. Most details of Radost's dress had been taken from the bank note.

The character whom Radost took to be Count Thurn himself who led the group charging the room was a vivid and enigmatically sketched figure. The artist who had illustrated the note had managed to render with just a few brief strokes the folds of destiny that lay within those features, or so Radost thought. Lucretia had to agree with him.

Actually, Lucretia found it a lot easier to go through with the sex if she entered into the fiction herself. She found herself imagining at the actual moment of penetration that she too was involved in the scene of defenestration, jumping away and falling out of the high window on the bank note and into the moat and safety. As Radost laboured away above her, she, a tiny figure on the note, no more than an extra in the scene, stepped across the lines of green ink and the figures spelling out 500 Crowns in gothic script and leapt of her own accord out of the window and into the ether. She looked closely at the 500 Crown note now and imagined herself even now off to one side of the scene in her brocade and veil, waiting to be summoned into activity. Then she uncreased the folded bill and placed it neatly on top of the others.

By the time Randy Hart returned from his artfully devised ploy, Lucretia was sat in her dressing gown with the notes from the envelope Radost had delivered to her all neatly counted out into piles.

—How was your randy-vous? quipped Hart.

—Profitable, said Lucretia and grinned towards her bank notes.

—Fancy, said Hart: And look what I've got. The keys to the kingdom.

He tossed Patak's keys down onto the Prussian blue of the counterpane, and then made to leap onto the bed after them and out the Hradcany window.

—No! laughed Lucretia, protecting her neat piles of bank notes.

—Classico! said cheery Hart and went across to the fridge for a beer instead.

# Chapter Five: Style Lord Gentleman

IN THE WEEKS leading up to Blackpool a number of things changed irrevocably.

Patak quit his job. He had tried swinging things round his way by inviting Rodkey for dinner and ordered a 'Luxury Supper' from Nemek the Caterers on Brodskinsky Bld: clear soup as first course, then special dumplings with spicy meatballs followed by apple strudel and washed down with a range of continental beers—not cheap. But Rodkey was having none of it. They were only on the first course when it became clear that Patak's request would fall on deaf ears. Already over dumplings Patak was formulating his resignation in his own mind—he would slam the resignation form down on Tycho Hedko's desk with the words *no hols no go Tycho* and working out the financial arrangements that would keep his head above water until the money from the Blackpool deals came through. By apple strudel time Patak was already reconstructing himself as a wayward and somewhat reckless game show executive, a kind of carefree and poetic soul, a bit like his mate Randy.

Lucretia had decided to have his advertising material published directly at the Blackpool congress and had sent the texts on to a top-level game show translating agency in Blackpool. Needless to say, that set Patak back by a few more Crowns. Still, Lucretia assured him that the texts would be waiting for them when they arrived in Blackpool, which took a load off his mind.

As for the ideas themselves, they had come on apace over recent weeks. Lucretia, Randy and Patak had spent a stimulating evening together over sea trout and white wine in the Paziz Hotel restaurant where they had beat out alternative developments for antagonism. What Patak had laid out before them was his punishment scenario. This stipulated that contestants had the option of taking the top money punishment option once they arrived at level two of the competition (i.e. after the commercial break). The punishment (or chastisement) option meant that if you failed in that part of the game, you not only lost what you had won in the show so far, which was of course shared out amongst the audience, but you were also punished in your life. Who knows how? Stripped of possessions? Your car? Even your apartment. Why not? And all these possessions were then distributed amongst the audience. Of course, all this had to be cleared with the legal experts. Lucretia was taking charge of this, as she was of so much. She was worth her weight in gold, that girl. Again she deemed it best to send away to Blackpool, where they apparently had top-notch game show lawyers who'd check through the fine print. Again big money earners, but Randy Hart's philosophy was that this thing had to be driven through to the end; in other words, if you've killed the wolf, you may as well bury it.

It was also during this particular dinner in the art deco reception rooms of the Hotel Paziz that Patak coined the nickname Lucky for Lucretia. It wasn't quite sure how he'd come up with it—amongst other things, he'd had a drink or two, he didn't mind admitting it—but suddenly he had apparently come out with it. Randy Hart had to point out to him what he'd said, he hadn't even noticed, he was coming out with words all the time now. Antagonism, chastisement, and now Lucky. He was firing on all cylinders. The three of them screamed with delight. Lucky! exclaimed Hart. *What a great name! Exactly right.* Lucky! Things were turning in his favour. Patak could feel it. As Randy Hart put it: *you're really on a roll, Patak. You'll be gobbling them up, come Blackpool.*

There was more stuff. The startling revelation was that the fellow Mandryka was larking about with Julia. It turned out that he was actually the same Mandryka as Mandryka's Chocolates and Chocky the Horse. To think of the number of boxes of chocolates that Patak had bought from Chocky the Horse. All the time subsidising, so to speak, Julia's eventual treachery.

In general, Julia's infidelity couldn't have come at a better moment, in that Patak was preparing to give her the chop anyway. In fact, it suited him to have the official version of the story with Randy and Lucretia as him letting her gently down, rather than vice versa. However, he remembered he'd already told Hart she was his ex and managed just in time to get the sequence of tenses right and the right kind of wistful distance into his account. When he'd told the story, Hart and Lucretia praised his sensitivity. In his fictional version of his rejection of Julia, he had told her that he was moving into the fast lane now and wanted her to think about whether she had the appropriate horsepower. The image worked with his auditors but jarred in his own mind. When he used the term horse-power, the image of Chocky the Horse emerged from nowhere. This was soon followed by the memory of the bull-necked Mandryka sunk in Julia's armchair and swilling on British sherry.

Never mind, he told himself. There were plenty more fish in the ocean. Und zwar, as the Germans put it, a certain Miss Lucretia or Lucky as she now was. Things, on that score, were hotting up. A glance here, a touch there, an interplay of smiles, the overlapping of laughter, the echoing of yawns and sneezes, secret empathies, the willingness to accompany, to be with, an affinity of mind, a kindredness of spirit. Nothing material. Nothing that would stand up in court. But lovers know, they know.

The first kiss was forthcoming. It was just a few days before they were due to leave for Blackpool. Patak was worrying. That was in his nature, as Hart told him often enough. He was a perfectionist. This time he was worrying about the documentation. Would the catalogues really be ready and waiting for them in Blackpool when they got there? Would they have time to go over them if they were there? Because Patak knew—he just knew—that things would be hectic when they got there. The atmosphere of the place, the thronging crowds, the bustle of top-notch business interchange, the aura of the place itself—Lucky had filled him in on this, she'd been there on a number of occasions over the years sorting out entertainment deals. All this meant that they wouldn't have the time to check through the catalogue for misprints. And why hadn't they sent the proofs over to Prague for him to vet? Heavens, he was paying them enough, wasn't he?

Lucretia let him rant for a couple of minutes until he ground to a halt. Then she came across to him, leaned up close and planted a kiss on his lips. Patak was silenced.

—That's merely professional, she said, but smiled. And added: For the moment.

Then she ruffled his hair. His hair was thinning on top but you couldn't quite say he was balding. She sauntered out into the beer garden of the inn where they were lunching together, and Patak, after he had paid the bill, trailed out after her. Since he'd quit his job, he was spending most lunch times in restaurants and taverns either with Lucky or with Randy Hart going over the finer details of the trip and sharing one or two splendid bottles of wine—his two colleagues certainly knew how to enjoy the finer things of life.

As the days counted away to the take-off to Blackpool, Patak found himself hardly able to contain his excitement. He found a short article about Blackpool in an old Czech encyclopaedia which he pored over time and again in an attempt to satisfy his thirst for knowledge of his glamorous destination:

'Blackpool. Resort town. England North West region. Sea-side holiday playground. Featuring Tower of Blackpool, festive English humour pastiche of Eiffel Tower Paris. Population 150,000 approx. Eleven kilometres approx. of sandy beach shore line. Many tourists in summer and at Holidays of Banks. September is period of lights, called illuminations, where many bulbs lighten up evening and night sky arranged in diverse patterns. Prestigious Blackpool Opera House hosts many international Western stars such as Frank Ifield and Ted Rogers.'

The encyclopaedia was a few years out of date—it had been compiled in the early sixties—but it was enough to give him a tantalising foretaste.

The night before the departure Patak took the time to sit down on his wide pink sofa and go over his finances.

Patak had peaked at 875,000 Crowns just before he met Randy Hart in The Golden Stag that time. He had signed over about 200,000 Crowns to Lucretia in preparations for the Blackpool trip. What with the catalogues and lawyers fees, it really mounted up. And those hotel suites didn't come cheap either. Then there were the allowances he was paying to Hart and Lucretia. Moreover, in the run up to Blackpool, what with discussion-lunches and stuff and all those fancy bottles of international wine, Patak found himself with his nest egg cut in half.

Meanwhile Julia was having fun.

Fun with Mandryka consisted of trips to small bars where over nibbles and drinks rapport was effortlessly set up with invariably cheery staff—with Patak it had been dutiful outings to one of three possible restaurants where despite Patak's faultless fidelity he knew nobody and nobody knew him; opera, where the move from apartment to theatre was so effortless that you might close you eyes in front of your dressing table mirror and open them in the plush dress circle surrounded by the well dressed and perfumed bit part actors with which you had furnished the snug of your imagination—with Patak any trip to the opera (always raucous operetta if Patak had his way) was spoilt by the fuss and worry of getting across town (bus, tram or rain drenched walk) from the tedious countdown at home to the second-rate fare at the theatre with Patak nudging her in the ribs every time the tune of a popular singalong rose up from the ruins of the paltry orchestra; cinema, which was engaged in spontaneously en route here or there, fortuitously taking in Europe and the New World, as well as the Far East and Russia, a tour du monde with constant blustery winds blown across the landscape of the imagination—with Patak it was Czech comedy and Czech comedy only, the rundown lots of the Barandov film studios used again and again and location shooting in Podoli, always in Podoli. Moreover, with Mandryka there were no circuses. With Patak it was a diet of cossacks and bears at least once a month and always in the same tedious routine.

The last time Julia had got Patak to accompany her to the Smetana Opera the whole thing degenerated into a farce. At the end of Act One when Patak insisted on buying choc-ices instead of the customary white wine and olives, he dropped his midnight mint over the edge of the balcony onto a woman's décolletage. Heads from the parterre cast immediately upwards towards where Patak was ogling down from the balustrade, who to make matters worse not only did not apologise but actually asked if any of the midnight mint remained edible. At the end of Act Two Patak could bear no more and went off to the restaurant to be sure of getting the reservation, as he put it. In fact, the opera itself—Pique Dame or The Queen of Spades—was somehow indicative of their relationship. At the end of Act Two Hermann was sure that he had found the winning sequence of cards that would make him a rich man, only for by the end of the play to be cruelly deceived, tricked by the Countess into choosing an Ace instead of a Queen. The irony was lost on Patak of course, as he was off at Gropius' downing his precious dark brew.

With Mandryka time became twenty-four open hours a day, it lost its monumental quality and became free flowing and easy. Activities drifted into each other, might be aborted or spontaneously extended and were not named as such. There was little naming. This was the crux of it. With Patak it was all naming. Fun was a series of immovable, defined blocks. Patak was forever fitting one pastime block up against the next, huge sensible squares as though fun were the construction of some terrible square edifice. For Mandryka fun was fun, construction came incidentally and naturally as the volume of lived fun filtered down. It seemed to root Julia's connection with Mandryka more in the real world.

Julia saw Patak in the street by accident a few days before the departure for Blackpool. She was just coming out of her sports club where she'd been working on the abdominals with a touch of buttock-work and there he was standing looking into a gentleman's outfitters on the other side of the street.

Julia crossed the road and tapped him on the shoulder.

—Good afternoon, said Patak, not deigning to turn. He had seen her reflection in the shop window.

—Are you looking for a new suit?

—In the spheres I move in you have to dress the part.

—Well, don't buy that one, will you. It looks awful.

They were both eyeing a pin-striped three-piecer with the label Style Lord Gentleman looped over a button.

—Czech tastes are not necessarily prevalent abroad, said Patak mysteriously, waiting for Julia to ask him about any trip he might have planned.

But she didn't. She was marvelling at the price ticket on the lapel of the hideous suit. For a moment she was stunned. The idea of Patak spending so much on a suit was such a novelty that she was dumbstruck. It had always been the other way round: she had spent the money and he had refused to believe it. Actually, Patak was thinking of buying a couple of matching suits, one for him and one for Randy Hart; a kind of unofficial antagonism uniform. And why not one for Lucretia too, a woman's suit in the same yellow dog tooth?

—Have you got the day off work? asked Julia. After all, it was a Thursday afternoon.

Patak guffawed.

—Oh, I don't work there any more. Hadn't you heard?

She hadn't.

—No, I wasn't going to be hemmed in by Rodkey and company. A time comes when a decision has to be made. We must learn to choose between.

Julia guessed it was the game show project.

—And how is the game show idea? she asked out of necessity. With the subject constantly winking at her it was difficult to avoid.

Patak smiled broadly.

Then he closed his eyes and nodded contentedly.

—Well, he said. Well.

Julia contemplated him in front of the gentleman's outfitters.

—Good. But don't put all your eggs in one basket, will you?

Patak didn't answer right away. A pause from the manual. Then he answered proverb with proverb.

—Less injury is sustained from falling from a horse than from falling from a donkey.

It was a piece of Randy Hart wisdom, not in fact a proverb but a fact. It was claimed—rightly or wrongly —that in falling from the higher seat on the back of a horse the rider had time to do a somersault in the air and land neatly on his bottom, whereas from a donkey you hit the ground on your face or your spine and so sustained greater injury. Randy Hart had adapted this old country saw into a life principle and Patak had taken up its heroic message, fatally confusing the concrete with the figurative.

The evening before the take-off to Manchester Patak received a call from Randy Hart. Patak had settled in for an early night. He had changed into his peignoir and was lounging around on the pink sofa with *Lives of the Romans Volume III* out on the rabbit hunt rug. He was flipping over the page on Justinius Superbus when the telephone fizzed out across the dimly lit evening apartment. As he padded across to unhook the receiver, it occurred to him how few calls he had received in recent months. Since the antagonism project had taken root, since Julia and he had parted company and he had quit his job, he seemed to have no friends left. Such were, he lamented, the tribulations of ploughing a lonely furrow in the field of light entertainment.

It was Hart.
—Randy! went Patak gleefully.
—How's it going?
—I'm just relaxing, taking it easy.
—Right you are.
—A final moment of reflection before the push.
—I know I know. All set for the take-off?
—Ten-thirty at Gate 15.
—That's right. Lucky will be there. Make no mistake about that. Only I've decided to take a later flight. One or two details to knock on the head before I get out there with you.

—But Randy, I thought we were all going together. We should all be going together. This is our project, all three of us...

—I know I know, but there are just a couple of things to sort out. I'll feel easier if I get it done here, then when we're out there, we can really focus on the job in hand.

Patak nodded sternly.

—Yes I understand, he said. Bend every sinew to the task.

—That's right that's right. But listen, don't worry, I'll be out next morning. Probably best if I leave next morning on the same flight. That'll mean you and Lucky holding the fort Friday night. How does that sound?

To Patak, that sounded good.

—I'd prefer you to come out with us, he said.

—And don't you think I'd prefer that too. Sunning myself on the golden Blackpool beach or bent over the financial break-down here in Prague? Which do you think I'd prefer? But business is business. It's got to be done.

—You're right, said Patak. Now isn't the time to get sentimental about what we've achieved.

—I knew you'd understand. Remember the Salon only starts on Monday. This weekend you'll just be getting into the swing. Do some tourism. Make yourself feel at home there.

—I wouldn't know what tourism to do...

—Visit the sights. The Tower of Blackpool and all those other things. There's masses of stuff to see.

—Is there? I couldn't find much in the encyclopaedia.

—Masses of stuff, repeated Hart. He wracked his brain.

—I mean, what do you think Blackpool's most famous for?

—I don't know, said Patak.

—Well, what do you think? There's the actual black pool, suggested Hart in a moment of genius, situated on the outskirts of the town.

—Oh, so there's really a black pool, is there?

—Of course, of course, famously guarded by a mythological dragon.

Patak nodded and looked across his apartment to the night sky beyond the window.

—Incredible, he said.

—So, the next time I see you will be in Blackpool, went on Hart.

Patak gulped. The time had gone by so fast. The moment of reckoning was imminent.

—Don't worry about it, said Hart. It won't be like you think.

Patak laughed. As team leader, it was important for him not to communicate any negative vibes, but behind his breast-plate his heart was starting to beat in a different way.

Patak packed. Three suits plus the two business suits in yellow dog tooth for Randy and Lucky (he was planning to spring them on his associates as a surprise). A panama hat. His business manual (it had become indispensable). The bundle of socks and underwear. Bathing trunks. A towel. Toiletries (a new aftershave called 'Wolvine' and an after shave balm from the same Wolvine range). The passport. Stacks of cash (the exchange rate was unfavourable). Two hundred newly printed business cards with four different letter fonts and an emblematic sketch of the twin masks of Tragedy and Comedy.

When the two suitcases was closed, Patak poured himself a stiff vodka and sat done on his pink sofa. A parallelogram of light came through from the hall and laid itself out on the carpet of the living room. Otherwise, the room was dark. He sipped his vodka. It was a splendid moment. Yes, he thought, I have done all these things well.

When Patak and Lucky left Prague it was sunny. When the plane landed at Manchester Ringway Airport in England three hours later, the rain had set in. From the airport they took the so-called hoppa bus into the city centre where they waited to pick up the bus to Blackpool. In Chorlton Street Bus Station they queued with a line-up of elderly people. The bus pulled up at half-past-two. First stop, Manchester Ringway Airport.

Arriving back at the airport for the second time in as many hours, it was already as if Patak had known the spot for years. The airport storage warehouses and outhouses in the drizzle wore that bleak look of tired familiarity. At the airport the bus rattled about for about half-an-hour between terminals one and two whilst random officials stepped on and off sharing jokes with the two drivers—there was a driver change-over at terminal two. By 3.45 they were off. At 4.30 they stopped at a service café just outside Preston where Patak and Lucretia shared a much needed cup of English tea. As far as they could make out from the map, they had only come about twenty miles, but, as Patak knew from his old Czech encyclopaedia the English ritual of tea-time was sacred.

By 4.30 local time in Prague Randy Hart had almost finished up.

He had let himself into Patak's apartment at about eleven that morning. There were one or two little objets that his keen eye had taken a fancy to: a splendid set of antlers on the living room wall, an Illyrian vase (Randy had an eye for the right kind of art), the computer and an old rug depicting a kind of rabbit hunt. These he put in the corner of the back room before the men came.

The evaluator showed up at twelve on the dot and Hart took him through the rooms. What with the furniture, the pots and pans, the clothes and the linen, on top of the ornaments and books, not to mention the customary mod' cons' including washing machine and fridge down to the blender and the grinder, the juicer and the whisker, it all worked out at the tidy sum of 450,000 Crowns.

By 4.30 the men had taken the lot away and Hart was sipping a last celebratory glass of vodka as he admired his newly acquired Illyrian vase. He walked round the bare apartment with the fine wooden floor creaking underfoot. He opened the french windows and stepped out onto the balcony. The blare of rush-hour Prague met him immediately. He looked out across the brick coloured roofs, the copper domes and filigree weather vanes of the famous old city. Clouds had skirted in from somewhere. They were sliding swiftly across the horizon as if on tracks. Hart took out one of his Park Lane's and surveyed the scene. This was the kind of apartment he'd pick up one day when he had real cash. It was just the right sort of pad for bachelor living. On the outside facade of the block just next to where he was standing on the balcony was a huge face. Hart took a proper look at it. It was an angel. The wings extended down the sides of its body alongside floors two and three with the face up here level with the fourth floor. Hart smiled. *Classico*! he said and struck a match for his smoke on its blank stone eye.

From Preston on Patak was straining out of the window. The road was long and straight and inevitably at the end of it lay the lapping sea. All along beside the road the margins of the drive into Blackpool were bleak, as though Blackpool were beckoning only with its long fingers, drawing all comers into the mammoth dreaming city through a thick outer rim of grimness. The end of the road took on the aspect common to all seascapes; the gentle rise towards blue or in this case steel grey infinity.

The bus turned off the main carriageway and round a couple of kinks and suddenly they were out on the sea front by the Pleasure Beach. The bus stopped and a couple of passengers got out. Above them high in the air was the iron track way of a huge fun ride, and at the back of and beyond the heavy dentellerie of its sky paths a two-dimensional city of pink and white candy stripes. As Patak cranked his gaze upwards towards the swirling grey skies a trainload of passengers fled by plummeting dramatically down the iron sky track, all of them screaming as the car twisted in its ground ward fall. Lucretia laughed. Patak pressed his nose anxiously against the bus window on the other side of which the rain was starting to patter.

## Chapter Six: The Counting House

BLACKPOOL, its starriness, its eager smiling faces, its children and older people, its throngs, its wafts of chips and vinegar, its bubble gum pink, its litter, its red lights, its vinyl gloss finish.

Patak understood Prague instinctively; the way the jigsaw fitted and the function of each and every piece; even the way people behaved there seemed to make sense to him. Blackpool was no Prague. It was a riddle; the town was impossible; a town that should exist only in fable. On the one hand, the mammoth scale of the Victorian architecture that constituted the sea-front walls with its levels of promenades and elaborate range of shelters and band-stands stretching for miles upon miles; and on the other hand, the ramshackle and provisional quality of the rest of the edifice with its cheap two storey houses and crooked rows of shops.

It was a city meant to be viewed from one side only, created for the immobile and uncurious. The length of the Promenade which ran from the Pleasure Beach at the Southern end past South Pier, Central Pier, the Tower and North Pier then up further past the Metropole Hotel and the Imperial Hotel was the facade, one attraction deep, and as thin as credit card plastic. In front of the Promenade ran the trams and the three levels of walkway, the lowest being just up from the seawall. These walkways were where you were meant to stand.

But venture just one street behind the outer facade round to the back doors of the Metropole Hotel and the Tower Complex and the rows upon rows of hotel units with en-suite facilities called The Balmoral or The Albert and Victoria or The Queens, or the Merrie England Bar or Robert's Oyster Bar or the bingo units and there the unpainted and unformulated jumble of fire escapes and backyards with the hash of uncolour-schemed outlets and inlets told another story, covert and unfamiliar, but on an equally massive scale, the shadowy world of the threepenny functionaries of the facade.

When Lucretia and Patak got out of the bus they made their way up to the Front which came out onto the Promenade level with North Pier. The drizzle had stopped and there was a kind of sketchy sunwash emerging from behind an imbroglio of clouds. Along the Front men and women were sitting or lying on the concrete areas, many of the men shirtless and a number of the women in bikinis. Patak and Lucretia crossed over towards the sun-side of the walkway but the sun was not strong enough to cast shadows or to let them discard their jackets.

They caught the tram a couple of stops further North and got off at the Metropole where Lucretia had booked them in. From the outside it was a grand block in its own island of space between the sea front and the front facade at a point where the front facade turned back a little and created an extra margin by the sea railings.

—I can't wait to have a look at our suites, said Patak.

—The suites? Didn't Randy tell you? I don't think they're booked for tonight.

—What do you mean not booked?

—Well, we thought we'd wait till Randy was here for the suites.

—So where are we sleeping tonight?

—In the hotel. But just in rooms.

—Rooms.

—Yes, just rooms.

They stepped over the perron and into the foyer. Patak lagged behind admiring the plush carpeting.

—This is Bohemian lozenge, he said.

—What's that?

—The design. It's Bohemian lozenge.

Lucretia was already over at the reception desk, leaving Patak poking at the carpet with his round toe shoes.

—Bohemian lozenge, he went on muttering to himself as Lucretia spoke to the receptionist, a small man with a smudge moustache.

Patak eventually came across to join Lucretia at reception.

—Charlie, shouted the receptionist over Patak's shoulder. I've got two B and B-ers over here.

Patak turned round towards Charlie, a little man sitting behind a lower desk.

—Get your vouchers from Charlie, said the receptionist, his eyes already on his clipboard.

Patak felt he ought to pipe up:

—We shall be attending the Game Show Salon in the Winter Gardens, he said.

The receptionist lifted his eyes from the clip-board for a moment, focusing on the bell on his desk, and then looked back down to the clip-board.

—Is there perhaps a bar down here where the game show guests will be gathering? asked Patak.

—The Galleon bar's first on the right, retorted the receptionist dryly.

—Come on, interrupted Lucretia. Let's see the rooms.

—He was a bit gruff, said Patak, as he struggled with the cases up the stairs. They were heavy; he had the dog-toothed suits in there. Their rooms were only accessible via the back entrance of the hotel, which was a converted fire escape. As Patak walked up the aluminium staircase to the third floor with a view of Springfield Rd and its collection of bingo units and discount shops with everything under £1 and impressive ranges of sexual accessories, he read the sign that was valid for the back area of the Metropole only; 'Butlin's Metropole Blackpool B&B £20 a night per person.'

By the time Patak had hung his suits up in the rickety cupboard and attempted unsuccessfully to pull back the dust-ridden drapes on their half metre of washing line, it was seven o'clock and time to go out for dinner. He knocked on Lucretia's door along the corridor, but there was no answer. From behind the shower door in the corridor—the corridor shared the shower and toilet facilities—he could hear a stream of water, so he waited. After a moment she emerged in her bath robe. Patak looked in her eye for some hint of the notion that the griminess of the accommodation was not what they had been expecting, but no hint of recognition was forthcoming. He went back to his room and waited some more.

By eight o'clock they were striding along the Front. Lucretia had not changed into the yellow dog-toothed antagonisms suit he had bought her, which disappointed him a little. Still, it wasn't officially game show week yet. Patak decided not to mention it.

They turned into Talbot Street and a pub called The Counting House with a sign showing a playing card king counting gold coins out onto a tabletop. They sat down with drinks, Lucretia a whisky and Patak an English beer. It was astounding. They could almost be back in Prague drinking at The Stag chewing over the coming trip, but now they were here in Blackpool. It had all come so quickly. As Patak sipped his beer and looked round the bar he was trying to sink this realisation deep into himself. Otherwise, he knew the whole trip would pass by in the wink of an eye. He looked round the bar to take in the scene.

The Blackpool women were less exotic than he had imagined. Obviously they had just chosen this bar at random and there would be other more selective bars where the more sophisticated Game show industry people would be bound to congregate. But the type of women in The Counting House seemed thick-set, with heavy white arms like enormous slabs of mountain cheese and very large feet. Lucretia was the best looking woman in the place, though that was no surprise. Under her suede jacket Lucretia was wearing a halter necked top which left her muscular shoulders free. The interlocking arcs of her clavicles, shoulders and the lines of her top plunging down towards her discrete cleavage created a Venn diagram of resplendent allure. A crucifix affixed to a chain held tight round her neck created an intersection that focused Patak's attention downwards towards her breasts. Patak almost licked his chops with anticipation.

When they left The Counting House and started to look for a suitable restaurant, they found only one on the sea front: Robert's Oyster Bar. They peered in but it was completely empty. Most of the business seemed to be done through a flap which looked out onto the open air where people could could buy cones of take-away mussels. Robert was sitting behind the flap-up counter smoking a cigarette and reading a newspaper. Most people seemed to be eating Fish and Chips, which, so Patak had read in his guide, was the local speciality, best eaten outdoors with the sea air. So the two of them bought a fish and chips each from one of the many outlets and walked down onto the lower walkway of the promenade.

—In a minute, said Patak, why don't we walk over to where the Exhibition is being held and just see if we can have a look round to get our bearings.

—Fine, said Lucretia, as she licked the vinegar from her paws.

Patak was starting to worry. The reason why they had decided on getting there for the weekend had been to make contact with other exhibitors, but for the moment there was no sign of Lucretia knowing quite how to go about this. The Blackpool people seemed oblivious to The Game Show Exhibition. Patak had seen no posters. He had even tried asking around the hotel whether anyone else had booked in who was going to the Show only to be met by a blank stare from the receptionist, who admittedly had to be no more than a student brought in for the season who knew nothing of the prestigious events of the month.

They walked back into the town from the Front, past the looming night presence of the Tower—it was now night time—and through the deserted shopping centre towards The Winter Gardens, which was the exhibition centre where the show was to take place.

Patak brightened up on seeing the Winter Gardens, which was a splendid arcade of bars and exhibition rooms attached to an ornate Opera House where they were playing a show featuring Little and Large (important celebrities, clearly) and a Tribute to the Three Degrees. Patak remembered it was in the Opera House that his encyclopaedia had told him that Frank Ifield and Ted Rodgers had played to standing ovations. Clearly Little and Large were comparable prestigious turns. The Exhibition rooms were all closed, but Lucretia found a poster advertising the Game Show Fair, which was to be held in the Empress Ballroom. Patak scrolled down the poster for clues about the fair:

\* \* \* \* \* \* \* \* \* \* \* \* \* \* \* \* \* \* \* \* \* \* \* \* \* \* \* \* \* \* \* \*

A host of family entertainment ideas!

For professional entry only. No admittance to the general public.

Professional salon for family entertainment game shows.

\* \* \* \* \* \* \* \* \* \* \* \* \* \* \* \* \* \* \* \* \* \* \* \* \* \* \* \* \* \* \* \*

In fact it was hardly a poster. Just a typed sheet. Patak had to admit it was something of a disappointment to see such an insignificant and rather grubby looking sheet placed behind a glass window as the sole advert of the forthcoming proceedings.

At least he was glad about the general public bit. No admittance to the general public. That was fine by Patak. Professionals only. Fine too. Patak had finally managed to effect his exit from the spheres of the uninitiated. Family entertainment. Where had he heard that term before? Family entertainment. He knew. It had been Mandryka. That buffoon had used the same term the day the two had met in Julia's apartment. What a coincidence the elephant man should harp on the appropriate term.

To get a feel for the place they slipped into the Prince of Wales Bar where a man with straggly long hair and the waxen complexion of one who has known high abuse was entertaining the drinkers with a medley of tunes on an electric guitar interspersed by a number of jokes. Above the racket Patak tried to turn Lucretia's mind towards the Exhibition.

Patak was coming to understand the important role played by Randy Hart in the commercial duo Lucky-Hart. Without him she seemed unfocused. That could have just been her nature of course, but Patak understood that the job of motivation was now incumbent upon him.

—What do you think our best policy should be when we get into the exhibition on Monday morning? he asked, trying to focus his churning brain.

Patak had to talk loudly over the din of the entertainer.

—I think you should man the stand while Randy and I go out searching for prospects. The important people know that if you've got a project for sale you won't be shy about coming forward.

That was more the kind of talk he was expecting from Lucky.

—Yes. That's right. I'll man the stand. But I'll need those catalogues. Where on earth are those catalogues?

They were supposed to be ready for us. You told me they were being prepared…

It was true about the catalogues, Lucretia realised. She had said they would be waiting for them when they arrived in Blackpool.

—Don't worry, don't worry, Monday morning at the exhibition…

Patak was suddenly up-in-arms. He'd completely forgotten about the catalogues. He'd even forgotten what he'd put in them.

—But what if they're not there…

—But of course they'll be there. I've worked with Sammy before. He won't let us down. But he won't be coming up from London till Sunday night…

—But I thought he was based in Blackpool, you told me he was based here at the heart of the industry…

Patak uttered these last words about the heart of the industry somewhat sheepishly. In the surroundings of the Prince of Wales Bar, with the over amplified voice of the entertainer fizzing in his ears and the other non-Game Show Exhibition preoccupations of so many other punters around him, all the stuff about the heart of the Game Show world was beginning to turn insubstantial in his mouth and come out like porridge.

—Well, yes, this is where he works mostly, but a lot of the shows transfer all over the world and the communications hub is in London. Obviously, he's a guy who has to move around a bit.

Lucretia brought her hand up to Patak's face and stroked him on the flushed cheek. But it wasn't just the catalogues that were troubling him. There were the lawyers too. Wasn't he supposed to be having a meeting with those Game Show lawyers? The week was suddenly beginning to look very empty.

Patak collected himself.

—When have we scheduled the meeting with the lawyers for? he asked.

Lucretia took a sip from her cocktail.

—Oh, the lawyers, she said. Later in the week. I can't remember which day exactly. Thursday or Friday.

He was quiet. Thursday or Friday seemed a long time away. Now he was worrying about the catalogues. Sammy had said they'd be here. Who was Sammy? He'd never heard that name mentioned before. What right did they have springing a new mask-head on his already fevered imagination?

Patak didn't know what to think. Who was Sammy? An image suddenly flashed into his head. Lucretia and Sammy, a tall fair muscular anglo-saxon, involved in high sex jinks. Patak tried to dispel the image from his mind, and the stab of jealousy that accompanied it.

Patak complained of indigestion. Lucretia was solicitous and said they should go back to the hotel and she'd rub it better for him. Since they had arrived at the Winter Gardens she had become much friendlier. As the evening drew on and the disturbing news about the catalogues and the lawyers had come out, her attentions had intensified. As they passed beneath the shadow of the Blackpool Tower, the possibility was looming that she and Patak (or Patacake as she had now suddenly taken to calling him) were about to consummate what had been becoming increasingly inevitable over the last few weeks. They turned out onto the blast of the sea front and Lucretia locked her arm into his and pushed up close towards his ample and protective flank.

—The thing is I don't remember very well what I put in that catalogue now, he said as they climbed the back staircase at the Metropole up towards the luminous sign marked EXIT which for some reason had been put on the wrong side of the doorway. As they stepped onto the uncarpeted boards that led towards the back, formerly servants, stairs that catered for the B&B section of the Metropole, Lucretia slipped her hand under his shirt onto the mat of his hirsute chest. One way or another, the catalogue would sort itself out now. Patak put his trust in the shadowy figure of Sammy, a new matchstickman in his imagination. Learning how to delegate was one of the lessons his American Management textbook had been at pains to teach him.

Patak trailed up the narrow stairway and round the cramped stairwell—it was more a pit than a well—behind the raspberry scented Lucretia. He focused on the backs of her slim ankles. She was wearing a three-quarter length waisted suede jacket with the high collar pulled up over her small pixie ears. The collar covered the tactically cut nudges and tufts of hair that snuggled into the nape of her neck. At the turning of the stair the plane of the side of her cheek came into sight before he too revolved around the twist of the staircase. Her features were small, but set upon a large head frame with robust architectural lines across the line of the jaw, the slash of the cheek, the rivet of the brow. Turning up across the magnolia painted whoosh of the bannister, her face was a superficial delight of whirls and tucks upon an inner masonry of no-nonsense beams and blocks.

On the landing they stopped and faced each other. Lucretia produced a controlled smile. Out of shyness, Patak tried to pull attention away from all intimacy.

—I hope Randy'll be ready for action when he gets here, he said, focusing mainly on his own toes.

—Why's that, Patacake? Are you disappointed in me? asked Lucretia.

His eyes refused to meet hers.

—In you? No. It's just Blackpool.

—Are you disappointed in Blackpool then?

He thought. He looked up and set his eyes on a square inch of Lucretia's cheek just below the revolver butt angle of her left cheek-bone. He wasn't disappointed in anything. His thoughts were just swimming into a different pond. Blackpool was a huge, uncaring scaffolding of provisional thoughtlessness and a difficult space for intensity. The mind looked to be distracted here. He was having difficulty getting to grips with the place. It was a place with a splendid frontage and an unofficial backyard; Patak had noticed that within minutes of arriving in the place. Its fraudulence was part of its nature. He was troubled. He had not come prepared for skulduggery.

—Not disappointed, he said. Just unbalanced for the moment.

—That's without sampling The Big Dipper, she said, probably smiling.

Patak etched a brief smile. He had understood something about Lucretia now. Not a big thing, and still not anything he could easily define. It was something to do with the rhythm of her conversation, the manufacture of her riposte, the way it opened up lines or closed them down, like the shifting of points on a railway track. He had settled the elements of her technique in his mind.

Albeit a technical aspect only, the mastering of this particular shape relaxed him, and from here it was a simple operation to move with her into her bedroom and rebegin a chat-up procedure that he had established many years ago and (he realised) never quite forgotten. Why! Patak had a whole range of woman experience. Remember those days when he used to switch girlfriends as easy as his monthly travelcard on the Prague Travel Network. Vanina; Tanja; Audrey. Who else had there been on that string of paper dolls? And now here he was clipping out another one with those nimble scissors of his.

They went through motions. At the back of his mind was the sense that this was one of the things he had been paying for over the last few months. He had paid her a small salary, plus all those meals and drinks. What had he seen for it all? Very little that was concrete. The application of her conversational technique; the chance to bend his mind to other subjects in company. The business of the Game Show idea was an elaborate fantasy he was paying to try and realise. In a way, Lucretia was part of the same operation. He had paid for her, hadn't he? A slide of Lucretia got up in game show finery comprising sequinned gown and golden envelope frolicking behind a lectern slipped through into his mind. It was true. She was a kind of call girl, a gold clad escort service.

She flapped his tie out of his jacket.

—I think I need you to stay with me tonight, she whispered sweetly in his ear.

Patak started to sweat.

—Indeed, he answered.

They moved into her room, she gracefully, he tripping over the carpet. His tongue of flimsy fringe flopped up and then down onto his mainly bald pate. She averted her gaze.

—Patacake, she said, helping him out of his highly worsted jacket. A whiff of underarm stink wafted up as his arms shrugged the garment off.

She smiled the short, economical smile of the professional call girl and began to undress.

Patak took one step backwards and began to undo the buttons on his shirt.

When she had got down to her underwear, which (Patak noticed) was crimson coloured, she slipped in between the sheets where she lay still.

Then Patak got into the bed beside her. He too kept his underwear on, as though it were one of a series of tacit rules that Blackpool lay down.

She was immediately breathing steadily, as if asleep. Patak waited. He cleared his throat a few times. After about twenty minutes he turned closer to her so that his knee was touching the backs of her legs. She remained immobile. Ten minutes later he moved his shoulder up against her shoulder blade. Only after about an hour did he try touching her with his hand. He rubbed her back a little above the bra-strap in a friendly kind of way, as if he were rubbing some ache better or patting a dog. Lucretia remained immobile. Her breathing remained steady.

He decided to take his mind off her. There would be plenty of time for further intimacy. What was the rush? About two hours later he managed to get to sleep.

In the night as Lucretia slept, Patak was aware of two distinct sources to the sounds that sifted in. From behind the bedstead and the back of the bedroom wall where the main carcass of the Hotel Metropole was massed with its multiplicity of dramas within its many rooms and suites came the indistinct noise of wheeling and dealing, a kind of mumbo jumbo issuing from the innards of the place that sounded a like the enactment of a black ritual. While in through the window from the back streets of the nether city behind the facade of the sea front with its smells of beer and sudden illogical displacements of men and women, a wurlitzer played into the deep dimensioned night.

Randy Hart arrived next day. He bowled into the Metropole with a new trilby in his hand and his air tickets peeking out of his top pocket. Patak and Lucky were waiting for him in one of the deep reception hall sofas. When he stepped into the vestibule Lucky leapt up and rushed across to embrace him. Hart put one arm round her back but he kept the trilby hand free to create enough aura space around them. Patak wandered slowly over.

—Randy, he said, smiling and nodding.

Hart held out the wrist of the trilby arm, which Patak shook. People in the hotel lobby were looking round. A newcomer had arrived. Clearly the husband of the woman and partner of the other, distrustful looking man in the ridiculous yellow dog-tooth suit. The sun was coming in through the glass doors and bathing them in a veil of light. For a moment the tableau was transfigured. Patak's heart leapt joyously to his throat. Everything was possible. Hart was engaged, attractive, voluminous suddenly in the Blackpool hotel. Things would sort themselves out now.

—Patak, friend! he said and smiled deeply.

They were all laughing in the sunshine.

—No time to lose, said the newcomer. I picked up a message from the printer last night...

—Sam... said Patak.

—Yes Sam, said Lucretia.

—Sam, repeated Hart. Yes, is it? The printer. Yes, Sam. Yes well fortunately I was there and got the message...

—Why didn't he phone here. Doesn't he know we're in Blackpool this weekend? asked Patak.

Hart pursed his lips and shrugged his shoulders.

—Whatever, he said. Whatever...

—What does he say? asked Lucretria.

—Well, that's just it. He wants us to go down to London to see him this weekend. He can't make it. So we'll have to pick up the catalogues ourselves. So I've got tickets on the next train down to London for me and Lucretia. I thought you'd better stay here and show yourself around a bit, he completed, turning towards Patak.

—I see.

—And actually, said Hart, looking at the watch on his trilby wrist. We have no time to lose if we want to get that train.

—What! You don't have to go straight away, do you? said Patak, disappointed to have Hart picking up his suitcase again.

—Aren't you going to check in first?

—Well no, it might be that we'll have to stay the night down there. It depends on our timing. I already cancelled my room for tonight. We must get going. If we miss the connection to Liverpool, we'll be in trouble we'll have to take the boat.

—The boat?

—Yes. The Liverpool-London boat, which is slower.

Then there were farewells. Lucretia and Hart dashed out to the taxi, waved through the window. They did not want to have to catch the Liverpool-London boat. They left the business partner standing alone in the vestibule. All was quiet once more. Patak went back over to the lobby sofa and plumped down into it. The upholstery gave out a sad yelp as it took on his weight.

That evening, which was Saturday evening, was a difficult time for Patak. He wanted to be constructive, but he didn't know what to do. He tried phoning Hart and Lucky on the mobile, but their phones were switched off. He had equipped the three of them with mobile phones so they could keep in touch with each other at all times. What was the point if they switched them off?

He went along to The Winter Gardens to try and look at the exhibition rooms once more. Saturday night was ballroom dancing night. Patak paid his entry and spent an hour watching elderly couples negotiate the polished floor of the Empress Ballroom. At one moment he found himself sitting next to a line of unaccompanied, middle-aged ladies, who asked him for a waltz. As it seemed harder to refuse than accept, he found himself acting as dance partner for a quartet of eager, business-like dance enthusiasts for the rest of the evening. The waltzes he managed to carry off more or less adequately but the Latin American numbers, which happened to be the particular favourites of the ladies, demanded elaborate leaps of the imagination and a range of sudden skips and hop-scotching that were certainly not out of the textbook. All the while Patak kept the beer rolling so that by the time the ballroom clock read ten, he was beginning to try out a number of moves from text-books of his own invention.

Just after ten the ladies left and Patak left with them. When they emerged from the ballroom, the four women wanted him to go on with them to a 'Bingo Nite' but Patak declined the invitation and said good-bye to the women, who, they said, would be in town all week and were staying at The Seaview B&B up north by Gynn Square. Patak pretended to make a mental note of the address and slipped away as the foursome started up a rousing chorus of a football chant that Patak himself knew (in a Czech version with somewhat lewder lyrics) from the terraces at Sparta Prague.

Patak came out onto Talbot Square by The Counting House—his old haunt—and nipped in there for another pint. As he stepped over the threshold past a couple of tuxedo clad bouncers, he looked up to the painted sign of the playing card King of Hearts with his eyes cast down in a melancholy look at the gold coins that he was counting (counting away, Patak presumed) on an oak brown banqueting table. Who was this king and what was his story?

The people of Blackpool were again out on the town. Patak recognised one or two slabs of cheese from the previous night. There was a ferocity with which the men and women here seemed to pursue the enjoyment of their leisure time. From the yelps of delight, the shouting across the saloon bar and the peels of uninhibited laughter, you would take this to be a bar for regulars in some frontier town of the new world rather than a playground for the gilded youth of Western civilisation. Patak, who had already had four pints, supped cautiously on his beer. In comparison with these young people, there was an awkwardness and prudence in his manner that was horribly out of place. Of course, these people were younger, less fashioned in the ways of the world than Patak, but at the same time he was aware of his need to ape this rough engagement in things and find that same savagery in his bargaining at the Game show exhibition on Monday. As Patak observed the antics of the indigenous people, he was beginning a period of mental steeling for the ordeals to come.

He tried following the workings of the conversation between the party beside him.

Ray had been fooling around with Mick's sister but Mick didn't care. Mick laughed and slapped Ray between the shoulder blades. Ray's pint tottered. Everyone laughed. Ben said something and everyone nodded. Dan tried to talk but was ignored. Mick said something and sniggered. Phil and Chris didn't hear what he'd said, so he repeated it. Geoff took issue with it and Rick said Oh no! Everyone laughed. Ben told them all to fuck off! Sam went off to get pints in. Dan went off to help him. Phil said something as Dan sloped off to the bar. They all watched Dan's long back at the bar. Mick said something about his sister again and Ray said fuck off!. This time Phil and Geoff and Ray laughed. It was complex and unfathomable.

Patak watched them through the brown beer of his pint. Behind the liquid their faces swam and sank.

As he was coming out of the pub after last orders at eleven o'clock, he looked up and down the boulevard where groups of youths were now transferring from pub to fish-and-chip-shop and then to discotheque. A hundred metres further up the promenade, crossing into the Blackpool Tower Experience with its range of bars and nite-clubs, were Randy Hart and Lucretia. In a moment they had disappeared inside the rust red complex. On top of the five pints of beer Patak was loathe to believe his eyes. They were supposed to be in London sorting out the catalogues with Sam.

Patak walked up to the entrance of the 'Tower Experience'. A row of alternate green, pink and orange light bulbs around the ticket booth were flashing off and on. He tried to peer up the wide stairway towards the gloom beyond the ticket booth, but Hart and Lucky, if it really had been they, had dispersed into the powdery dark.

Patak paid his £8 entry fee and stepped in. When he had pushed through the glass doors he found himself in a thronging foyer with a host of other fun seekers all weighing up their options. Across the foyer was a long bar and at each extremity the two entrances to the ballroom, which to judge from the thumping rhythms issuing from it was for tonight at least doubling up as a disco. When the doors swung open the greens and reds of the strobe lighting flashed out.

Lucky and Hart must have got back from London earlier than they thought and looked for him at the Metropole, Patak told himself. He would probably find a note slid under his door when he got back. No matter how logical it sounded, somehow he didn't believe a word of it. Suddenly, looking around at more eager participants in the events of the pleasure operation, Patak felt desperately lonely. He looked across at the long bar and felt little inclined to imbibe another beer. The disco floor attracted him even less. In the maelstrom out there he would never find Lucky and Hart. He walked half-heartedly across to all the noise but stopped halfway. He was dead tired. It probably wasn't them he'd seen anyway.

When he got back to the Metropole there was no note. No matter. He wasn't up to an extension on his night out anyway. The wurlitzer was still sounding out the back of the Metropole. Patak closed his eyes to its dreamy rhythms.

Julia and Mandryka had arrived in Blackpool for supper time. They had decided not to go out but dined on one of the balconies of their suite at the Metropole Hotel. The rooms looked out onto the sea where a pale bronze sun, cold and merely decorative, was slipping down over the edge of the world. They were sipping champagne and swallowing oysters, whilst in the drawing room Schumann's Liederkreis Opus 39 based on the Eichendorff poems was playing in the Fischer–Dieskau version. Only isolated shards of the twilight tones drifted out onto the balcony. Below them the grey green sea beat against the sea wall and up above the drink gulls hovered, cried and bent their dull rubber eyes on the two lovers.

Night fell definitively. They stayed late out on the balcony wrapped in shawls and overcoats looking across to the moon. Gradually the sounds of the night disappeared. The organs and cries of revelling. Just as they were about to turn in, a final couple, a man and a woman, both uproariously drunk and caught in gales of laughter about a Liverpool-London boat, arrived back in the Metropole foyer. But they were a distant sound, a tiny disturbance to the balance of the night from many, many light years away.

## Chapter Seven: The Metropole

PATAK WOKE up late the next morning. There was a vacuum cleaner going in the room next-door. He leapt up and padded out into the corridor in his stocking feet—he slept in his socks on chilly nights. A young man in a white tee-shirt with the inscription You Can Do It was pushing a hoover up and down the one free square of furnitureless carpet in Lucretia's bedroom. Her things had gone from the room.

—Where's she gone? asked Patak.
—Who's that?
—The girl who's in this room. Who else, for heaven's sake? barked Patak irritably.
—No. Nobody's in this room now till two o'clock this afternoon. I'm getting the sheets cleaned and all that, though I don't think they were slept in last night.

The bed was untouched.

Patak went down to the reception at the front of the hotel, where the receptionist said that Lucretia had moved out of her B&B room and into a suite with another gentleman yesterday evening. The receptionist didn't know what time as he hadn't been on duty, but Patak presumed it must have been late on when they got back from London.

It all made sense. They had agreed to move into the suites on the Sunday. They had perhaps thought best to move in a day early. There was no point Hart getting all settled into a B&B room for just one night. Patak asked for his suite, which was sure to be just next to their suites, but there seemed to be nothing booked in his name. He got the receptionist to bring the manager in and check who was booked into the suite next to Hart, but it was someone called Jackson. Hart must have used another name instead of Patak's to reserve the suite, but where, if not next-door, had he put him. The manager refused to allow Patak to scan the guest list for some coded version of his own name. On the off-chance Patak asked the manager to look up the name Antagonism. Was there anyone booked into the suites with that name? If there was, then it was he, crowed Patak with a triumphant trill. But there was no Antagonism. The closest was a Mr Charles Anthony. As a final favour the manager agreed to check if there was a room booked under Game Show, but the closest was Mr Gamelon. Then Patak remembered that they had planned to book him into the top suite in the hotel, The Victoria Suite, but the receptionist was adamant, the Victoria Suite had been occupied last night by another couple, also from abroad.

Patak phoned up to Hart's suite but there was no answer. Why should he be in? It was getting on for midday. Patak had missed breakfast, so he stepped out into the bracing air. In Blackpool, Patak had noticed, *bracing* was always placed in front of the word *air*, sometimes even hyphenated as in *bracing-air*, as though it were a single entity. This fusion of adjective and known was also in *fresh-croissant* and *Henry VIII-breakfast platter*.

He looked around for a place to walk to. There didn't seem to be anywhere he hadn't explored. Everywhere seemed to lead back to the same two or three hubs of interest: the Tower Complex; the Winter Gardens; the Hotel Metropole.

Patak's impression of Blackpool was of some huge single mansion with paper thin walls separating the different rooms. They were more in the nature of flaps than walls which could be slid one way or another and spun round to create apparently new spaces and alter the angles, so that when you blinked you were in a new unit of the Bluebeard's Castle.

In all of these ever-changing rooms were a variety of mostly interchangeable one-dimensional characters named Dan and Ben, Ray and Rick, Geoff and Sam, Mike and Mick who all had heads a third the size of their bodies with jutting jaws and thick necks. They switched into action when you clacked one of the flats into a new wall and revealed a new space: laughing uproariously; pointing over their shoulder with their outsized thumbs; indicating towards other spaces with a rolling of their bovine, nicotine coloured eyes; grinning literally from ear to ear.

It was riotous slapstick that could reach levels of frenzy when the huge mechanism of the Blackpool mansion was turning full pelt. At the back somewhere were the cogs, the levers and cranks, the monstrous machinery that ran it all. Patak suspected there was some secret part of the town he had overlooked where the headquarters were situated, an abandoned warehouse within which a team of white-overalled technicians kept the whole gothic operation spinning.

He walked along to the North Pier where a crowd had gathered around a booth. Patak pushed his way into a place where he could get a view of the sketch.

On the front of the booth a rectangle had been cut out of the candy striped linen and a couple of glove puppets were performing. Squawking parrot-like voices were coming from within the booth. Above the cut-away stage a broad ribbon was pinned across with the words 'Awdley's Punch and Judy Theatre'.

Patak watched the show for a few minutes. As far as he could make out there were five characters: Punch and Judy, a Police Constable, a Crocodile and a Devil. And five props: a link of sausages, a sausage pan, a stick used for wife beating, a gallows and a devil's fork.

He soon had it worked out in dramaturgical terms. Bliss; Order; Physical Threat; Metaphysical Threat were the four co-ordinates.

Act One went from Bliss to Physical Threat as Punch and Judy prepared to eat sausages before strife set in and Punch decided to beat his wife.

Act Two introduced the Police Constable and the Crocodile and delineated the movement from a return to order with the threat of gallows looming for Punch to the threat of extraordinary anarchy with the crocodile eating both sausages and Policeman.

And in a surreal Act Three the Devil sent the Crocodile packing to hell and had his own ears boxed by Judy wielding the sausage pan.

It was fantastic Antagonisms, wonderful dramaturgy with three levels of physical and metaphysical interpretation. And how the Blackpool audience lapped it up. These were people ripe for Antagonisms. They were the perfect vehicles for the new brand of Punch and Judy that Patak's game show had to offer.

Patak felt happy to be engulfed in the crowd. It warmed him. The last couple of days had been hard going. Not quite in the way he had imagined before the trip, but in a more basic kind of way. Being away from home had affected him in a way he could never have believed. Blackpool had been a harsh and unwelcoming kind of place so far. He missed things. Insignificant things: small domestic appliances he was used to; the bulky presence of the arm of his sofa next to his ribs; the peculiar smell of his apartment which was that delicate compound of the goblin self and the familiarised alien quality of his personal effects. Here in Blackpool there was none of that. He was basically alone. His own goblin smells stuck to him. An unpleasant, bloody taste was seeping up from his gums into his mouth. His arms felt too short and his clothes hung poorly on him. He could find no use for his surroundings; the Tower Complex and the pedestrian precincts, it was as if he could not make out what they were for. His room with its stranded sink unit in a bed space was an alien presence he could not assimilate. As part of the sink unit there was a great deal of exposed plumbing on which his eyes seemed to be forever resting with monotonous regularity.

Now he was enjoying being part of a crowd and looking around at the collection of variegated bystanders when he spotted none other than Julia standing on the other side of the crowd with that fellow of hers, the Chocky Choco fellow. What on earth were they doing here? In the midst of this group of strangers, they looked oddly out of place.

Almost immediately Julia caught his eye. She grinned broadly. Patak was unaccustomed to seeing such an uninhibited display of glee from her that it almost crossed his mind she might be smiling at someone else. He hardly knew what kind of expression to fork back at her. He kind of shrugged. He saw Julia nudge the Chocky Choc fellow and then the two of them started edging through the crowd towards him. Patak focused on the playlet as they approached him.

The Devil was creeping up behind Mr Punch and the children in the crowd were shouting out warnings to him. *Behind You!* they cried. *Behind You!*

—Patak, said Julia, tapping him on his shoulder.

They slipped out of the throng. The Choco fellow accompanied them.

—You remember Mandryka, said Julia.

Patak clicked his heels in a kind of Austro-Hungarian salute and said 'sir', not looking at him the while.

Mandryka merely smiled.

—What are you doing here? asked Patak, taking on the exasperated strangled tone that was customary when he talked to Julia.

—We're on holiday. Remember. I knew about this place before you did.

—Nonsense.

—I did. I told you there were adverts for Blackpool at the Lenski Travel Agency.

—You said nothing of the sort but what matter!

—Quite. Anyway, we're all here now, so you'll just have to accept it, won't you?

—I have no intention of not accepting it.

The Chocky fellow was still smiling with affected serenity like a kind of psychiatric nurse.

—And how's business going? laughed Julia.

—It starts tomorrow, said Patak and gulped.

—Well, good luck. Where are those partners of yours I heard so much about?

—I seem to have missed them this morning.

—Well, I hope you find them again. I suppose you don't want to eat with us tonight.

Julia turned to Mandryka.

—That'd be all right, wouldn't it?

Mandryka nodded and chuckled.

—The offer is most kind, riposted Patak, whipping up a fine lather of sarcasm. However, I fear I shall be somewhat preoccupied this evening.

—Of course, said Julia. Still, if you change your mind, we're in the Metropole Hotel. It's that big one up the promenade there...

I know which one it is, countered Patak irritably. I'm actually there myself. In one of the suites, of course.

—Oh, which floor? We're on the fifth floor. Ours is called The Victoria Suite. We have a magnificent view. Where's yours?

—Oh, I can't remember now. You know the view makes very little difference to me. At the present time, as you can well imagine, I'm fixed pretty much on my own business. I keep the curtains on the outside world well drawn.

—A true professional, said Mandryka, opening his mouth for the first time.

The man's insinuating, unpleasant tone came back to Patak. What on earth did she see in a man like that? He was an ogre. Just look at his big balloon of a head. It was a wonder some child didn't carry it off on the end of a string.

There was applause. They turned round and saw Judy clanking the sausage pan on the devil's head. The play concluded. The audience moved away and two puppeteers came out from behind the booth. They went over to the hat that had been laid out at the front to see what their takings were. One of them pocketed the takings with an inelegant and unstylised dip of the shoulder.

—We'd better be off, said Julia after a moment's pause. We're going up to Fleetwood on the tramline. Mandryka's booked us in for lunch at the North Euston Hotel there.

—Yes, me too. I'd better be on my way. There are all kinds of details to sort out before tomorrow.

—You'd better find those errant collaborators of yours, eh! said Mandryka. They're probably scoffing ice cream somewhere.

—I will, said Patak and was already moving away, actually walking backwards.

—See you about then, said Julia, waving.

—Yes, yes, said Patak impatiently and stumbled on an uneven plank on the pier but skilfully managed to regain his balance.

He turned, still in a military mode for some reason, and hastened back to the hotel.

Julia and Mandryka watched his figure stalking off on the windswept sea front for a moment. Julia hardly knew whether to laugh or cry.

—Poor Patak, she said. He's just so nervous.

Mandryka said nothing and just looked out into the distance.

Randy Hart and Lucky had not been to London. They had taken the taxi up to the Euston North Hotel in Fleetwood and eaten a meal of jellied slab ox tongue with a glass of stout as entrée followed by buttered new potatoes, small sweet peas, fresh chopped cabbage, fine young carrots and braised black beef in rich gravy with further glasses of stout as main course followed by a strong pudding of damson sponge soaked in rum and smothered in caramel custard. At three PM this was washed down with half a bottle of Highland Clan scotch whisky, after which they sat watching elderly men rolling black cannon balls up and down a green.

At five o'clock they strolled across to the tram and rode back into Blackpool. Hardly able to contain their giggles they sneaked back into the Metropole. They picked up the key to their suite and were escorted up by luggage boy and lift boy, before diving onto the foamy bed with its elaborately trilled headboard. Half-an-hour later Hart crept back to the B&B end of the hotel to pick up Lucky's stuff. As he padded past Patak's room with the floorboards creaking like in some cheap B-movie, he was overtaken by another fit of the giggles. But Patak did not surface and the transfer went off smoothly.

They slept through the early evening. At ten o'clock they went via an ice cream parlour to The Tower Experience Discotheque where they danced the latest Blackpool dances—soon picked up—until two in the morning.

As they were getting back to the Metropole the giggles overtook them again. Hart chose the moment they were climbing the Metropole steps to come out with his latest imitation of Patak, this time recreating his shambling walk before turning round and fixing Lucky with one of Patak's so-called *from under the brow* looks. He called the impression *Patak on the look-out for the dragon guarding the famous black pool.* They screamed with laughter as they stumbled into the foyer. It had been a long day.

Next day was Sunday. No sign of Patak when they came through the foyer at one in the afternoon, but when they were on the way back to the hotel after brunch at the 'Imperial', they spied him sitting on a bench looking forlornly out to sea. They were scurrying back to the Metropole when Lucky came face to face with one of her clients from back in Prague. Seen here in Blackpool the vision almost took her breath away.

He was accompanied by a smartly dressed woman with auburn hair and had just stepped off the Fleetwood tram. He was unmistakable with his big crumpled head and lopsided features. It was client number three, the one whose name she could never remember, not Waldner, not Radost, but the other one. Lucretia stood stock still.

Client number three too was clearly embarrassed by this apparition from his nether life surging up from the streets of Blackpool Great Britain.

—Come on, said Hart. What are you playing at? Let's get back to the hotel before he sees us.

Mandryka was ignoring them but glanced furtively across when he heard this, but it was clear that his whore's partner was referring to someone else. He put his arm to the waist of his companion and eased her off in the direction of the Metropole.

—Let's just wait a second, said Lucretia, and wheeled Hart off to the side.

—What's up? He's going to see us. Come on, let's get back to the hotel, was Hart.

—Shush! Listen. That guy who just got off the tram.

—Yeah! Funny-looking. Did you notice how big his head was? Guys like that should be forced to wear hats at all times.

—It was that third client of mine.
—Who?
—The one whose name I can never remember. Client number three.

—What? What's he doing here? Was he the guy who told you about Blackpool in the first place.

—I don't know.

She realised now that he had been the one who had first mentioned the subject of Blackpool. It was when she had been dressed up in a long, sequinned number and he had told her she was just right to be hostess in a quiz show.

—They're going into the Metropole, said Hart.

—Great! said Lucky, her eyes rolling upwards.

—Never mind, said Hart. What does it matter?

—No, said Lucky. It just gave me a shock, that's all.

Hart sniggered.

—Not half as much of a shock as it gave him, I'll bet. I mean, that must've been his wife with him.

—Yes, I suppose it was.

They started approaching the hotel gingerly. When they came inside the foyer the client was nowhere to be seen. However, they were suddenly confronted by Patak.

—Crikes, Hart whispered to Lucreia. It's out of the net and onto the trident.

—Patak, friend, he said. Where've you been?

—Where've you been? said Patak, his voice too loud for the Sunday afternoon foyer—he had not spoken to many people over the last twenty-four hours.

—When did you get back from London?

—Last night, said Hart.

—Well, I saw you'd moved out of the room, said Patak addressing Lucky.

—Yes, we moved into the suite, she answered.

—I thought as much. I tried to sort out what name you'd put me under, but those idiots at the reception desk wouldn't let me look at the guest list.

They went over to the reception and tried to sort out Patak's suite. But there was clearly some mix-up as there was no Patak down and Hart was sure he'd used that name.

—It doesn't surprise me, said Hart, shaking his head. They messed up the reservation for Lucky as well. She's in with me.

—But this is scandalous, said Patak. We paid for three suites, didn't we…?

—Of course we did, was Hart, quick to settle any doubt on that score. The thing is, they're all booked up. There are no suites left.

At this point Patak laughed, bowed and shook his head. Hart looked unsurely at Lucky.

—Well, said Patak. I should have known it would end up this way.

He was laughing. Hart and Lucky laughed too.

—The three of us sharing a suite. Well, I suppose it's only fitting. The three of us in it together.

They laughed some more.

—As it's been from the start, said Hart.

—Give me a moment to check out of my room and I'll be up with you, said Patak.

Smiles all round while Patak explained to the receptionist that he was moving into the suite with his two friends. As Patak was explaining it all to the dim-witted receptionist he felt a tap on his shoulder. It was Julia. Chocky Choc was standing at her shoulder again like a guardsman.

—How's it going? she said.

—Fine, said Patak.

—Problems with the suite? said the Chocky Choc fellow, leering intolerably, or so it seemed to Patak.

—No, he snapped back. No problem at all. Just clearing up one or two details.

Lucky and Hart stood stock still, working it all out.

A minute later they were all standing round together, all five of them: Patak, Lucky and Hart, the client who was being introduced to them as Mandryka and his wife with the auburn hair who was being presented as Julia, an old friend of Patak's.

—So you're the partners we've heard so much about, said Julia.

—Indeed we are, said Hart. Just for the business side of the operation. The creative side is all Patak's.

Lucky and Mandryka smiled.

—He found you again, did he? He seemed to have mislaid you this morning, said Mandryka.

Everyone smiled.

—How strange for five people from Prague to all meet in the same hotel in Blackpool, said Lucretia mischievously. It must be fate.

—There's no such thing as fate, said Mandryka.

—Well, coincidence, then, said Lucretia.

—There's no such thing as coincidence either, said Mandryka. Lenski Travel was pushing Blackpool this year. That's all there is to it!

—Don't snap, dear! whispered Julia into his ear.

—But, piped up Patak. You forget that I and my two collaborators are not here on tourist pleasure.

—Indeed I do, replied Mandryka. And yet I wonder if the Blackpool Salon was mentioned in the Lenski Brochure.

—Absurd! said Patak. It's a professional salon. Not for members of the general public. If not for one of my collaborators who's been working for years in the game show business I might not even have spotted it myself.

—Indeed, acknowledged Mandryka. Well, as a mere outsider, I bow to your superior professional position. You and your associates.

With a sidelong glance at Lucretia he made to lead Julia away.

—Well, we shan't keep you. I'm sure you have a lot of preparations to make, said Julia.

Au revoirs were made as quickly as the bonjours. Patak reproduced the Austro-Hungarian heel click he was reserving for Julia these days. He let Mandryka and Julia sail up in the lift and followed them up with his two collaborators two minutes later.

—Was that your ex? asked Randy Hart in the lift, as Patak stared at the floor numbers.

—My ex? Whatever makes you think that? My ex? Why on earth should she be my ex?

—No reason. I just thought maybe she'd sneaked along here to try and catch up with you. I mean, you did look guilty. And I know you said you let her down gently, but letting down is letting down.

There was no hiding things from Randy Hart, and, in any case, what was there to hide? Patak was unable to erase the smile as the lift door opened.

—The poor kid, he said. What can I do about it if she's so stuck on me?

—I got to hand it to you, said Hart. You're a dark one, you are. I mean, that girl, she's not such a bad looker you know. Quite a nasty curl to her lip, that one.

—Do you really think so? said Patak, now at Randy's heel as the tireless collaborator advanced along the corridor towards the suite. Lucretia followed a few steps behind, smirking and shaking her head.

—I suppose she is quite a looker in her own way, repeated Patak, trying to familiarise himself with the idea.

—Yes, said Hart. Hair, eyes, teeth, legs... she's got the lot.

It was true, thought Patak. Hair, legs, teeth.

—Well, he said, grinning modestly. I suppose so.

Hart put the key noisily into the lock and spluttered a little to cover up anything Patak might be saying, wrapping up another aimless little conversation with the half-wit.

—So this is the suite, said Patak, gradually reanimating after twenty-four hours of sorry self dependence. The idea that Hart thought Julia was a looker had cheered him up no end. He went into the bedroom and bounced up and down on the bed. In the drawing room Hart and Lucky countenanced each other sadly to hear the bedsprings trill under the impulsion of Patak's dreary mass.

—Not bad! came his voice from the bedroom.
—There's the sofa too, said Hart buoyantly.
—Is that where you slept last night?
—Mmm, said Hart.
—What's that?
—Yes. Yes. Very comfortable actually.
—Good for you, said Patak and came out of the bedroom.

Hart and Julia affixed more smiles.
Patak clapped his hands.
—So, how's about those brochures?
—Have you seen the view from the balcony, Patacake? said Lucretia and went to open the french windows.

A gust of air came blowing in from the sea, a mixture of salt air, chip fat and candy floss.
—Bracing-air, said Patak.
—Come out onto the balcony with me, she said. Randy, why don't you go down and bring up some beer and sandwiches?

Randy obeyed. Patak stepped out onto the balcony with Lucretia.
—Listen, she said and pushed the french windows to so that they were out there alone with the elements. Randy doesn't know about us, you know...

Patak made a self-satisfied pleat of his mouth.
—You would have thought he'd have guessed, she went on. It must be so obvious. I can't keep my eyes off you. I don't know how you keep your composure.

She locked her arm in his.

—You know what it's like, said Patak. A man can be blind to many things. He probably has a ridiculous schoolboy crush on you himself.

—I just wanted you to know. Tonight, no matter what happens, Randy'll be on the sofa and we'll be in the bed. I think I'd better make that clear with him as soon as he gets up.

—Nonsense, said Patak, ever the gentleman. That's my role. Leave Randy to me.

Lucretia snuggled up close. She put her hand up to the back of Patak's head and twiddled with his side-burns before strumming on his ridiculous big ears.

After a moment Hart came through the door with a tray of sandwiches and three beers.

—Room service, he chirped.

Patak disengaged himself from Lucretia's embrace. It was absurd him feeling guilty abut this romance. There was no reason for it, yet he couldn't stop himself feeling that he was somehow betraying his mate Randy Hart by taking up with Lucretia in such an unashamed fashion.

They came in off the balcony.

—So, what about those brochures then? he said, trying to avoid the issue.

Lucretia was having none of it.

—No, I think we'd better tell him, she said sternly. Randy, Patak's got something to tell you.

Hart turned unflinching, trustful blue eyes onto Patak.

Patak coughed and stuttered.

—The thing is, he started. The thing is that Lucky and myself... while you were still back in Prague... in the evening we had a drink or two and ended up...

Patak didn't need to finish.

—You and Lucretia... together, said Hart.

Patak nodded. '

—So, said Lucretia, who was turning out to be just as tough a customer as Patak had hoped. So tonight, you'll be on the sofa again Randy and Patak and I will be...

—Of course, of course, was Randy, blushing and looking down to his shoes but quick to help them out of their embarrassment. Good old Randy Hart! Why should it bother him anyway? He had no stake in the matter. Maybe he was the other way inclined. The thought hadn't crossed Patak's mind before, but if Hart did prefer tacking against the wind, it would make a lot of sense. That immediate, friendly rapport was suddenly cast in a new light. Not that Patak had anything against them, far from it, but it was as good to know where you stood with this kind of thing. He resolved to quiz Lucky on the matter at the next opportunity. For the moment a beer and a... what was it?... pilchard and onion sandwich would go down a treat.

The exhibition organisers had arranged the game show proposers, as they were named, in an inner circle. Beyond them, in an outer round, were the various services that feed into the show such as accounts consultants, set designers and maquettists, agents, production companies, transit companies, lighting designers and stockists, freelance presenters, audience animation specialists and so on.

Beyond the two concentric circles at the top end of the Grand Ballroom was the Long Bar serving a range of hot and cold drinks and buffet snacks throughout the day.

When Patak arrived with Hart and Lucky in tow at ten o'clock on Monday morning, the organisers—whose visible manifestation was three middle-aged ladies in flowered blouses and red sashes—were placing the signs designating the various game show proposers on the tables of the inner circle. Patak walked from twelve o'clock round to eight o'clock where the Antagonisms sign had just been put in place. He checked on the titles of the other proposers: Sporting Assassins; The Staircase; Dare or Die; Word Count; Hop Scotch; Blind Alley; Poll Prey; Friend or Foe; Tarte à la Crème; The Monster Game.

A number of proposers were setting up cardboard models of the sets or pinning up photographs onto the backdrops. On the Dare or Die stand someone had already set up an array of flashing lights and popped in a cassette of eerie ambience music. Various video screens were being installed. A slide show was already in progress on the Blind Alley stand.

The morning was to be given over to setting up the various stands. At lunch time there was to be an informal welcoming buffet and sherry party. The actual business was to start in the afternoon with the manning of stands for informal contacts. Tuesday was given over to the formal presentations of the various projects, each project to be given half an hour. A little rostrum was at this moment being set up at the bull's eye of the two concentric circles. Antagonisms was down for 11.30 AM. The rest of the week would then be spent in following up the interest shown in the initial presentations

Patak was sulking. The brochures had still not arrived from London. Hart and Lucretia had sped down there on what had turned out to be a wild goose chase. Sam the publisher had left information with his transport manager to keep the brochures in his offices for Hart and Lucretia to pick up, but the transport manager's junior had never got the message and packed them off. In theory, they should get to the exhibition by Tuesday, but Patak found himself fearing the worst. So little of what had been promised, of what he had already paid for, had actually materialised.

While the other exhibitors set up their stands, Patak sat darkly behind his table twiddling his thumbs and chewing on his inner lip. Hart and Lucretia were sharing a cup of coffee at the Long Bar. Over the shoulder of the guy at The Staircase stand, Patak watched them both. Observed from behind like this, they were two alien animals. Patak knew he could trust neither of them. Deep subterranean doubts that he had blocked out for so long had erupted to the surface when he had heard about the brochures. It was now suddenly apparent to him that the whole organisation of the trip was up the spout. Moreover, it even occurred to him in moments like this, when he could see them only from behind or in shadowy profile and they could not maintain their eye contact power over him, that they were no more than a couple of jumped-up impostors. Hart for one had the Mala Strana background. Patak's parents, like all good East Bank parents, had warned him of the Mala Strana wiles. Never trust them, they have much to gain and naught to lose. He could hear his mother's guarded tones even now.

Patak closed his eyes and tried to think. But at this stage it was hard to get your mind straight. His thoughts automatically scampered towards a place of refuge. Into his mind's eye came the picture of his mother's house in the countryside near Pec. It was bathed in plum red and wine gum yellow as though set in a leaded window. Beyond it were layers upon layers of meadows undulating gently away into the distance. It was a place where the world of light entertainment held no sway.

Randy Hart and Lucretia had two cups of coffee and a couple of fresh croissants up at the Long Bar. Patak was in a foul mood. At about eleven o'clock Lucretia went over to the stand where Patak was still sitting staring blankly out at the activity going on all around him. By now what was to turn out to be the official anthem of the exhibition, a Tina Turner number entitled In the Name of Truth, was blaring out over the loud-speakers. Henceforth it would be played at any lull in the proceedings and for the next week, and indeed for many weeks that followed, it was forever playing itself out on the glockenspiel of Patak's inner ear, bringing back a melody of painful memories.

—Shame about those brochures, said Lucretia.

Patak nodded and bit deep into his lip.

—But they should be here by tomorrow, she added and ruffled his hair.

Then she hitched her skirt up and sat on the corner of the table, looking out in the same direction as Patak towards the Long Bar to the place where she and Hart had been sipping coffee. Hart had now gone via the Gents toilets back to the hotel. She looked out with Patak in a gesture of solidarity. Patak looked up towards the back of her jaw. He could see her eyelashes batting and the curls of her ear but the rest of her face was turned away from him.

Lucretia's mobile rang. It would be Hart. Who else could it be? She muttered into the mouthpiece for a moment. After a couple of minutes she eased down off the table and went for a little walk around the exhibition, she said, though Patak soon saw her slipping out the fire exit of the ballroom. When she had gone, Patak surprised himself breathing a sigh of relief and jumped up from the table with a sudden resolve. In the next half-hour he found a printer who agreed to produce an edited version of his presentation in an eight-page Antagonisms brochure for the next day.

That night Lucretia insisted on Randy Hart being allowed to share the bed with them. I mean, she said, Poor Old Randy! Why should he get a crick back? It seemed churlish for Patak to disagree and, besides, it was a wide enough divan. She called it family size, and Patak was too downcast to insist on anything else. Lucky slept in the middle between the two men.

For a long time Patak couldn't sleep. Lucky was sleeping on her side. She had turned her back on him. And she and Hart seemed awfully restless.

## Chapter Eight: Our Kind of Laughter

SINCE JULIA and Mandryka had met with Patak and his two associates in the foyer of the Metropole Hotel, the trip had seemed to lose much of its zest. Julia could not understand why, but Mandryka had turned broody on her. He had insisted on going out for an evening walk just as Julia was getting into a bath so that she could not accompany him. At the time Julia thought nothing of it. When you spend a week with someone, it's only natural for the spontaneous moments of communion to be tempered by the desire for moments of solitude. That seemed natural enough. Mandryka would come back refreshed, innerly resourced and raring to go. But he didn't come back for a long time.

Julia lingered over her bath; stepped out when the water had cooled; applied her range of creams, powders and scents; tried on each of her five outfits in turn in front of the mirror; plumped for the purple dress with the wholesome schoolgirl ribbons and the plunging neckline; took her time choosing her accessories (dainty crucifix and dinky wine bottle ear-rings); and drank two tonic waters from the fridge. Still no sign of him. Julia plonked herself down on the sofa and flicked on the television.

Mandryka was troubled. Although he personally had no great cause to look out for Patak, the fool was nevertheless an old friend of Julia's. One of his so-called collaborators being his whore almost certainly meant he was the victim of some scam or other. Whatever else she was, she was a competent performer in all aspects of the games of deceit and seduction. She had to be to operate in the scenarios Mandryka mapped out for her. He recalled with a thrill even now how she had acquitted herself in the French maid scenario. The way she had gazed at him through artfully placed wayward strands of her chestnut brunette wig had been just the ticket. In the genre she was unsurpassable.

However, were Mandryka to reveal his suspicions to Julia, it could not be long before the cat was let out of the bag and the source of his information questioned, which would mean owning up to his weekly visits to a 10,000 Crown an hour whore, an admission that he was loath to make.

Mandryka purchased a bag of chips from off the prom and sat down to eat them. The wind was springing up from the Irish Sea and starting to roll abandoned sheets of the morning newspaper across the walkway. He looked along the promenade to the North Pier with the posters for 'Anthony Rowley: Our Kind of Laughter!' in red and yellow. He finished the chips in no time. Mandryka was a big man. He needed fuelling. When he was with Julia he tended to eat about half of what he was used to putting away. He'd find himself chomping through salads and picking round lightly garnished *médaillons de veau* when what he really wanted was a sack load of potatoes and a flank of beef.

The streetlights were flickering on, through from pale raspberry to barley sugar orange when he strode back into the hotel and asked for Patak's room number. The room was not booked in his name but the receptionist knew of the strange trio in the fourth floor suite, not least because Patak was forever leaving the message that if anyone from the Game show Salon should come looking for him that was where he was. Mandryka journeyed up to the fourth floor in the lift.

The door was opened by Lucretia. A banana body scent she had bought on the Front wafted out of the apartment. The two looked at each other for a moment shorn of disguises. She was chewing gum. Mandryka set his jaw.

—What do you want? she said.
—Where is he?
—Who?
—Who do you think I mean? Chocky the Horse. The clown in the yellow suit.

Mandryka pushed through into the reception room.

—He's not here, said Lucretia as she trailed behind him back into the room.

—Are you here alone? asked Mandryka.

At this moment the bathroom door swung open and revealed Randy Hart with nothing but a small pale blue towel with the word Metropole on it covering his ignoble parts. Mandryka ignored him.

—What are you doing here? asked Mandryka, turning to Lucretia.

—We're helping Patak on his game show project, she replied, still chewing and affecting a casual languor.

—Yeah, said the almost naked Hart from the bathroom door.

—And what's that? said Mandryka.

—Antagonisms, answered Lucretia and blew a bubble with her gum.

Mandryka sat himself slowly down on the sofa. Hart looked anxiously across to Lucretia. Mandryka was such a large shaped man; and Hart was nude, give or take a loincloth. Hart reckoned that he weighed about three fifths the weight of the huge stranger.

—I hardly expected my mentioning the Blackpool Quiz Salon to my whore would lead to this, said Mandryka.

—Fate makes for strange bedfellows, Hart dared to quip.

Mandryka gave him a dark look.

—There is no such thing as fate, he said, speaking in a low voice. In any case, now there's nothing to be gained from accusations either way.

Randy Hart came out from the bathroom entrance onto the carpet, although it was not sure to him what he came out there to do.

—What we need to do, went on Mandryka, is wrap this thing up quickly for our mutual benefit. Now, I know this Patak character is a buffoon and I agree with you that whatever it is you had in mind he's got coming to him. However, being the gentleman I am, I'd like to clear things up for him and you.

—Clear what up? said Hart.

—Let him talk, Randy, said Lucretia.

—I'll pay you just to leave him alone. How about that?

—We don't understand what you mean, said Lucretia, keeping her voice bloodless so that it was clear to Mandryka she was interested in hearing more, albeit unwilling to fully own up to the scam for the moment.

—It's difficult for me to get cash, said Mandryka.

Randy Hart's ears pricked.

—It'll have to be cash, he said, almost losing his Metropole towel in the excitement of a cash incentive.

—I'll try and get you something by tomorrow. What about 100,000 Crowns for you to leave here and never see Patak again?

—200,000! said Lucretia.

—Impossible. 100,000 is all I could get my hands on out here.

—But I'm sure 200,000 is little enough for safeguarding your good name, noted Lucretia.

Mandryka tipped his wide, moo shaped head to one side a little like an oversized tomcat to reflect a moment.

Lucretia went on:

—And what about us, you and me? I don't suppose we'll be meeting up in Prague after this, will we? I need to compensate for a loss of revenue there.

—Right, said Hart to back her up, but without clothes it was difficult for him to assume a weighty presence in the room. He made a kind of aggressive shimmy from behind his Metropole towel.

Mandryka shifted the angle of his head again and glanced across at the naked man. Then he brought his big fleshy hand up to his forehead to paw away a fallen lock. The heavy stasis of his features snapped into action.

—Fine, he said, pushing up from the sofa: 200,000 it is. 100,000 in cash tomorrow morning. Also a cheque for 100,000 which you can pay into your account when you get back to Prague tomorrow afternoon. We'll sort this out at eleven o'clock tomorrow morning.

—Agreed, said Lucretia. We'll be holding Patak's hand at the Winter Gardens before his presentation. Come there to the bar at the Exhibition Centre.

—The Winter Gardens it is.

And Mandryka left without looking behind him. Lucretia chewed vigourously on her gum and Randy Hart scratched behind the Metropole towel at his pubic hair.

At 11.25 on Tuesday as Patak was going through the last of his hundreds of rehearsals of the text of his speech, he was broached by a rodent-like German guy with a greasy ponytail and a baseball cap. He was not drunk but it was as if he was. He was singing the theme tune to Family Openers, a popular quiz show of the day, and doing a crab like dance shuffle from side to side pistonning his elbows backwards and forwards. He sidled up to Patak at the Antagonism stand and one unfortunate jerk of his elbow too many sent Patak's plastic goblet of coffee toppling and frothing Cappuccino Italian Blend spilling all over his dog tooth suit. Then, two minutes earlier than scheduled, applause sounded through the hall. They were announcing Patak's name. He was on.

Patak cleared his throat and took a sip of water. Around him the audience was waiting. The other game show proposers were shifting uneasily. He had seen a few of them in action that morning. Laughing Jack Crowther from The Staircase, a game that gave participants the choice of two staircases to climb with various tasks on various stairs. Crowther, who was presenter as well as ideas man, had called the journey up the stairs a stations of the cross on the road to riches. Nebb Pleasemann, the representative from Norwegian based Word Count, a dry and unengaging personality whose presentation lasted only seven minutes. Word Count was, after all, tried and trusted in Norway, he had said. Brenda O'Madden from Hop Scotch, an Irishwoman whose accent was completely incomprehensible to Patak but who managed to get a trail of laughs by referring to characters famous to British television audiences.

Mixed in among the proposers were the agents and TV company representatives, the executive producers and deputy heads of light entertainment, the production companies and *Game Show News* reporters, all milling together as Patak spoke, sipping at coffee, whispering in ears, smiling or looking irritable, yawning and looking for chairs, moving forward or sloping out of the hall, tapping numbers into their mobiles, the lot of them a shimmering organic unit not unlike the football crowd at Sparta Prague.

Patak started up.

—My ladies and gentlemen, it is with enormous pleasure that I bring to you this game show concept by the name of Antagonisms. It is a radically different type of game show concept which I feel sure will create revolution in the universe of game show light entertainment.

To make this radical nature of Antagonisms clear I shall first expound to you, most honoured guests and fellow game show professionals, what I see as the present underlying structures of game show culture in European world.

The game show, as it exists at present, consists of a set; the programme producers; a presenter (invariably male) and his invariably two, invariably female assistants; the participants who are often in competition one against the other; the studio audience; the television audience; and finally, though not of least importance, the rest of the world.

And now, most honoured guests, some words about these elements.

The set is of the type emblematic and functional. It consists of various accessories, for example the clock and the exclusion booth. These accessories are both functional but also emblematic of underlying myth: the passage of time; the desire to belong to a group of initiates.

This latter concept of inclusion as opposed to exclusion is a useful way of looking at the other elements in the game show armoury.

Included are the presenter and his assistants; they animate, umpire and adorn the game.

Included also are the participants, who are the game protagonists, and the studio audience.

Excluded, but only because they are the gods, are the programme producers who are the ultimate arbiters.

Excluded too, but in a different way, is the television audience.

Excluded, totally, is the rest of the world.

The exclusion of the television audience is ambiguous. They are also—are they not, most esteemed audience?—in a sense included. In fact, they are on the fence, half-in, half-out, and this is how the tension is maintained and the ratings kept agreeably high.

A simple demonstration of the centrality of the inclusion-exclusion axis is the use of catch phrase, which reiterates at various points throughout the show the importance of knowing the culture, or, as you pleasantly say in English, being in the know, the know being a club to which we all aspire.

Such is the Game show as we know it today.

And now, most illustrious ladies and gentlemen, to Antagonism.

Antagonisms is a new type of game show concept. Instead of the merely convivial antagonism set up between two competitors or between the competitors and clock with the studio audience as a benign observer of the struggle, Antagonism proposes a conflict not only between the two competitors but also between studio audience and competitors. In a nutshell, if the competitors win, the audience loses; and, in that same nutshell, if the competitors lose, the audience wins. So that what is set up is a true play of forces, a true drama with true protagonists.

This idea of a play of forces or what I call force lines is central to the notion of the game show. What I call a force line is no more than a stake in the action, an invisible electro-magnetic thread extending between the participants, a tension generator, ladies and gentlemen.

What characterises the present situation in game show culture is the almost total lack of force lines between the various participants. And this in a genre where force lines are paramount. Think of the television audience. What do they have at stake? Nothing. They do not participate. They merely spectate. Witness the enormous popularity of lottery draws from east to west of Europe. A T.V. audience is crying out to participate in the play of forces.

Antagonism is about drawing up these force lines. Here is the present state of affairs. Between the T.V. audience and the studio audience there are no force lines; between the studio audience and the contestants there are no real force lines; between the producers and the presenter there are no visible and performing force lines.

Antagonism as a concept is about setting up this web of force lines, so that every shift in the skein produces a tremor that will unhorse one participant or other in the network. The interplay of forces must be that tight. This, ladies and gentlemen, is Antagonism. All we need now is ideas, feedback, initiatives and finance to create in reality this new generation of game show.

As Patak was talking he was half consciously scanning the hall for Randy Hart and Lucretia, but they were nowhere to be seen.

In his mind's eye their images had transformed. Previously he had seen the pair of them from the back or from behind, lit from beneath or form some oblique angle so that there was never a clean, untarnished view of them but they were half seen, shadowy figures. Now the image of them had changed. They now appeared as wholly static transfers burnt on the plaque of his mind's eye, or else as transfixed and sprawling woodcuts splayed out face-on for investigation. They had been stilled and iconised for examination. Nor light nor angles could touch them. In fact, the image that flicked through his mind now as he eyeballed for them was the definitive one: they were the Knave of Spades and the Queen of Hearts; richly made-up, simply etched, two-dimensional, inscrutable, ghastly. In Patak's brain they were now complete.

Which was just as well, as they had scarpered. That morning they had followed him to the exhibition and hung around with him throughout the morning. Around eleven o clock just as he was going through a final muttering revision of his presentation, they moved away to the bar to give him the necessary peace and quiet. The last he actually saw of them was the familiar hunched position of Hart at the bar. He was holding a tall pint glass of beer. Lucretia was sipping on a glass of martini or gin of some kind. They were both talking to some huge figure with a square back and tall gothic ears. The next time Patak checked, just before he had his Italian blend spilt all over his lapel, they were gone.

The plane was leaving at 2.30 pm, which gave them plenty of time for the taxi to take them into Manchester airport. Whooshing along the motorway eastwards towards the airport, they totted up what they had made out of the business.

Aside from the months of allowances and the special Blackpool trip allowance with entertainments fund they had managed to negotiate and receive in advance cash payment, there was the matter of the hotel. Hart had, in fact, booked one suite in The Metropole for three nights and not, as he had informed Patak, three suites for a week. The saving on such an outlay was considerable. Back in Prague, the furniture, personal effects and accessories and the whole collection of bits and bobs from Patak's apartment had fetched a tidy sum. There was even the chance of letting the place to some desperate, unsuspecting party and getting three months' rent out of it, if they were sharp about fitting it in before Patak got back on Friday. He would surely stay out in Blackpool till Friday. And now, on top of all this, was the 100,000 cash premium plus the distinct possibility of getting the 100,000 cheque into their account before any mishap occurred.

The Mandryka cash payoff had come as a fortuitous bolt from the blue. They had been dithering about whether to try and eke further sums out of Patak or quit while they were still ahead when Mandryka had showed up. No doubt about it, the Gods were smiling down on them. All in all, there had been a fair packet of cash involved. Plus, the lark of the thing, which in itself had been no mean entertainment.

Back on the plane and downing the airplane tray fare of vegetable terrines, cheese and biscuit packages and dainty gateau slices, they had to admit, it hadn't been such a bad undertaking. No banks had been shattered, but they were better off now than a few months back. There was money which might just set them up for some solid venture in the future. And, barring accident, they would never see Patak again.

When Patak had completed his presentation he stepped down off the podium. The first face he met was that of the rodent-like German with the pony tail who had spilt his coffee all over his lapel. He was holding another plastic goblet in his hands. Patak backed away

—Greek, said the German. All Greek.

Patak was in no mood to face those who refused to come half-way to meet his vision.

—All Greek, said the German once more.

—Nonsense, said Patak. Perfectly understandable if you take the time to study the leaflet. And he stormed off back to his stand.

The murmurs that he heard throughout the day seemed less than favourable. One or two people were mildly approving and stopped by at the stand to pick up another copy of their misplaced leaflet, but in general there were few direct encounters with anyone that mattered.

From a cubicle in the toilets just after lunch he overheard a conversation about his theories no doubt pursued by a couple of urinating game show executives. One of them was talking about Manhunt, the show that set members of the general public out at large in the streets and employed a band of highly trained ex-secret service men to track them down. Exactly, said the other one, that's what our friend is calling antagonism and its been going on for years. Patak was half inclined to hurriedly spring forth from the cubicle with his trousers about his ankles and sprinkle the two execs with a range of his more original ideas there and then, but he deemed it an imprudent move and resolved instead to track down the cynical couple later on in the day in more conducive circumstances. Unfortunately, he was not quite sure who had been involved in the tête-à-tête and spent much of the next few days trying to unravel the enigma of the mysterious urinators.

Throughout the remaining few days of the conference Patak took to hanging out at the corner of the conference bar and listening in to the different conversations, from time to time angling a strategic little comment into the discussion. He would pipe up with comments like 'Antagonism factor 0.75, worth pursuing' or 'force lines poorly articulated, look again'. Since his presentation he had become a salon personality, a kind of conference mascot. His gauche infiltrations into private conversations were tolerated with the good humour that is habitually shown to harmless eccentrics. The frozen smile over the shoulder became a stock gesture of the conference, though a civility aimed more at keeping at bay an alien spirit than in integrating him into the discussions.

Late one evening when most of the participants had cleared away for the day he noticed a familiar face smoking a king size over at the long bar. It was Jerzy Grotowski, Head of the Prague network Light Entertainment Department and mastermind behind the awful Foolish Thoughts programme and the man who had never deigned to give him an interview. When Patak confronted him in their native Czech Jerzy smiled from ear to ear. *It was good to hear the old tongue again*, he said, and, he confided, in Blackpool he was calling himself Jerry Grogan, more mellifluous to English ears. *And what about the presentation?* asked Patak. What did he think about antagonisms? *It sounded very interesting*, said Jerry, although, unfortunately, the sorry state of his English didn't allow him to understand much of it, but was he not right in saying that it involved the presence of mobile phone strategies, and perhaps he would be best advised including unusual pets in the show, as they were set to become very big in Prague next season.

Hart and Lucretia had gone. When he got back to the hotel on Tuesday evening after the presentation day his things had been moved out of the suite and had been packed untidily into his suitcases and stored in a stock room in the basement. There were no suites left in the hotel, so Patak went back to one of the B&B rooms. He was fortunate enough in managing to get one with en-suite facilities.

Already by Thursday many of the stands had been packed away and many of the exhibitors moved on. He continued turning up at 9.30 when the ballroom doors opened, but when he was there he frequently found himself at a loose end and ended up spending hours at a time sat behind his stand reading a paperback Agatha Christie novel he had found on a rainswept prom.

On Friday lunch time, at the official closing of the salon, he packed up his few accessories with his leaflets into his briefcase and made a point of going round shaking hands with all those who were left in the salon—mostly organisers, although there remained a musical jingle composer who wanted to share a drink with him. Patak declined: he was already booked up for lunch. Which for once was true. Julia had bumped into him in the foyer of the hotel. She and the Chocky Choc fellow were flying back to Prague at four o'clock. Did Patak care to join them on the North Pier for a matinee show and a spot of lunch? Why not? It wasn't as if he had anything much to lose.

The matinee show was 'Anthony Rowley: Our Kind of Laughter', which had apparently been playing to packed piers all week. The show wasn't in the North Pier Theatre but in the Sun Lounge. When Patak arrived, Wurlitzer Ted was entertaining the assembly with a medley of old-time numbers. Julia and Mandryka had taken a table near the back of the hall and were sipping at drinks. Patak was invited to sit between them.

—What'll it be? said the Chocky fellow, all smiles.

—Beer, said Patak dully. He was tired. Blackpool, to all intents and purposes, was over.

The waiter was summoned. Patak was served.

—Cheers, they all said.

—I caught your presentation, said Chocky. Very impressive.

Julia looked at him.

—When was this?

—Tuesday, said Chocky.

—You never said you were going. Why didn t you tell me? I'd have loved to see it.

She was half annoyed that he hadn't told her but also impressed. Mandryka missed nothing. He informed himself of things and slaked his curiosity without her even knowing it. He was formidable.

Patak hardly believed he'd been there himself.

—I didn't see you, he said.

—No. I didn't want to put you off. I kept a low profile.

Patak shifted an inch of his beer. It slopped down his gullet towards his empty stomach. He didn't know quite what to think.

—An interesting and original preamble, I thought. I'd be interested to hear further details myself. I suppose you're turning investors away by now though.

Patak didn't know how to take it. He drank a solid block of his red beer. His narrow throat was opening to the stuff.

—Easy on the beer, Patak, laughed Julia. She'd never seen him drinking so resolutely before.

—I've acquired a taste for it, he said. And anyway, it's been a hard week, I can tell you. I deserve it.

—I'm sure you do, Patak. But don't rush it. We've got all afternoon, said Julia.

—Well, we've got all afternoon. Maybe Patak's got a meeting or two lined up, said Chocky.

Patak sunk his pint.

—No. I want to see the show, he cried, his face muscles relaxing instinctively with the down flow of beer.

—Another pint for the man, called Mandryka across the Sun Lounge. In the enclosed area Mandryka's heavy voice sounded like a set of hammer blows. Looking round for the oncoming beer Patak noticed that most of the other patrons were small elderly people, many of them with no teeth, some of them dozing with their mouths agape.

Up on the raised platform that was the stage a banner was stretched across with the words 'Travels with My Old Dad' daubed up on it.

—Where are your friends? said Julia. Perhaps they want to come and have a drink with us.

For a moment he didn't understand. Then the image of the Knave of Spades and Queen of Hearts slipped into his mind.

—No, he said. They've gone back. They had to hurry back.

A draught of the bitter lodged behind his Adam's Apple, threatening to trouble him with heartburn. Mandryka picked at one of the clams from the saucer.

Wurlitzer Ted completed his last number to a round of applause and disappeared round the back of a makeshift curtain. Almost immediately from the same curtain came Anthony Rowley—it must have been him—galloping onto the stage. Between his legs he held a pole with a wooden horse's head on the end of it. *Woah Dobbin*! he said, *Woah Dobbin*! Rowley was greeted with spontaneous laughter and applause from the old folk, who seemed to come alive with his entry.

Rowley was parading up and down the small makeshift stage, making lunges as if he was having difficulty keeping his hobby-horse under control and on the platform. He was a middle-aged man with leathery skin, wearing what was clearly a wig, a mass of dense brown thatch on his head that sat rigidly in place as he skipped up and down on the pole.

—Yes well, me and my old dad we got around I can tell you, we didn't half get around, he started:

> Places we saw places all right. You wouldn't believe half the places we saw... wouldn't believe it, you wouldn't. The continent, we lengthed and breadthed it, we did, though never any place so la-di-da as this here pier. We used to dream of playing at a place like this, up in front of nobs, 'cause (how can I explain it to you Madam) you was nobs to us madam and proper uns too. We was poor, you see. Poor but

proud, that's what we was. We had our pride, ain't it. 'Cause even the poor's got its pride, madam. Oh yes, that's one thing my old dad taught us. That's one thing he left in his testament, so to speak, ain't it. And I'll tell you a little story to that effect, if you give me a mo'.

We'd be on the road in the Loire country. Now that's in Frenchie land for your information, madam. Now your Frenchie's a fine lad though not worth your Briton. Give me two Frenchies for one of our lads, ain't that so madam. Still, we'd be crossing the land in our country wagon with our old horse Dobbin, ain't it Dobbin. Woah boy! Woah boy! I got to keep him on the leash you know. He's left, right and centre, aren't you. Left, right and ruddy centre. And anyway, all of a sudden, out come a couple of these Frenchies. Masked they'd be. Black masks and muskets. 'Up hands!' they said. 'Up with them.' Anyroad, we couldn't really, 'cause I had hold of the reins and as for my old dad, well, I'll tell you what he was doing, he was having a slash out the side as we went along, 'cause that's what he liked to do, it was one of his preferred pastimes, so to speak, trailing silver trickles along by the wheel tracks. Oh yes, he was a creative man in everything he did, was my old dad. Sure, he had his habits. I ain't never said he didn't have no habits, did I now. I ain't never said that.

Now, funny thing was one of those Frenchies was a Blackie. That's right madam, tar-face and all, monkey eyes, spread out nose, a nigger, not to mince words. Don't ask me why, don't ask me how, but honest to goodness, swearing on my mother's grave, that's what he was. I saw it straight out; no mask could cover it up. Not the one he had on, anyway, 'cause I could see his blubby lips, ain't it. And any case, you hear it in the voice with a blackie. It don't come from the same place as a real voice. But that's evolution taking a wrong turn and not my business.

Don't know why I call it funny. Wasn't funny at the time, I can tell you, him and his musket trained on my old dad's willie-winkie. No blackie boys in here today I hope. Course not madam, just pulling your leg. Now where was I? That's right. We was proud folk, me and my old dad. Though my old dad's willie weren't so proud at that moment if I remember the look of it rightly. It's going back a bit you understand. My memory's not what it used to be, nor was my old dad's Willie, if I can picture it, poor sluggy thing it was. It puts a taste in my mouth just to think of it. Still, that was age. Yes, that was age and your darkie's no respect for a thing like that. Age, I mean, madam, so stop your smirking 'ain't it.

He'd even unlatched his black cock and... whoops a daisy dumps! I'll rephrase that one... He'd even cocked his black musket and aimed it. I could see his teeth through his blackie lips. And he was licking them. His lips. Imagine that! Licking them with his tongue. Red tongue, mind. Coral red, it was, if my memory serves. Almost licking the black right off. There'd be a fine thing.

Picture us! Piece out the imperfections in your mind, as the poet says. And my old dad's piece too, if you please. Well to cut a long story short, here's how it turns out. There's one of the highwaymen out at the back of the wagon rummaging for I don't know what. Any old knick-knack'll spark a Frenchie's fancy. While our friend the golly keeps his eyes peeled and his musket cocked, ain't it. But I'll tell you one thing madam, if you give me a mo'. Your swollen faced

Blackie ain't the quickest of thinkers. There's not much between the ears. You see, the head's so swollen up on the outside, there ain't no room left on the inside for brains bigger than walnuts. That's what the medicals'll tell you, mind, and not strictly speaking my business. But my old dad must've known it 'cause it was he who outsmarted the darkie, thinking like a young fellow of five and twenty, and not like some old bird of three score and ten like he was.

'Take anything you want,' he said. 'But don't nab my old pocket watch which I bought for a fortune in London Town all of thirty years ago.' Which was his way of saying: 'Say yer prayers, tar-face.' 'Cause I knew he was faking it right out and up to some scheme. It's something between father and son that. Sensation, if you like. And I knew it was some ruse 'cause the only pocket watch he'd ever bought was an old tin one from South Pier market which couldn't tell you the time of year let alone the time of day. 'Here,' he said. 'Just leave us alone and I'll willingly part with it. If I can only unclip it from my chain.' I should have known the blackie'd lose his head at this kind of offer. My old dad sensed it you see. Yes, he knew a thing about human nature did my old dad. He knew one thing, you see. That whatever greed we all have in our hearts, your Frenchie's heart can be sure to have a double helping. It's too strong for them, you see. They can't control their instinct. And that was his undoing, as it is the undoing of many a man not a gentleman.

So, the blackie trots round on his horse to help him off with his watch. And while he's tugging at the chain I can see what my old dad's up to, 'cause quick as a wink he'd looped a rope round the nig's ankle.

That's right, madam: the blackie's evil eyes were too preoccupied with the watch to notice what was going on. My old dad gives me the wink. I ups the reins and off we go. And off we go! Gee up there Dobbin! Off we goes, a-dragging and a-carting the dusky Frenchie along in the dust, knocking him this way and that. Dobbin needed no whip to tell him, did you Dobbin? That's right, we pulled him from his horse with the rope my old dad used for a washing line, and there was the golly bouncing up and down on the hard baked ground like so many Frenchies in the past have met their fate at the hands of wily Brits.

It was all over for the Frenchies in less than a minute. My old dad jumped down from the cart, cut the washing rope and left the Frenchie by the wayside. His friend took to his heels, or his horse's heels, 'cause he'd seen he was dealing with a couple of Brits smarter by half than your Frenchie.

Now ain't that so says I!

This final remark was greeted with a thundering response from the audience, echoing back Rowley's catch line in one voice: 'Ain't that so says I! Then breaking out into tumultuous applause and roars of approval as Rowley galloped round the stage on his hobby-horse.

Patak had finished his beer and was calling for another.

—Not much antagonism here, said Mandryka, smiling round at the rows of jubilant spectators.

By now Rowley had got a couple of members of the audience up on stage with him. There was an old man with his trousers round his ankles and a middle-aged woman belly dancing. It was the part where Rowley and his old dad meet the arabs in the desert countries. Now he was calling for two more spectators to come up and play the role of the camel.

—Fancy taking part? said Mandryka.

Patak poked his nose into his pint and looked through the brown liquid towards the table-top, where he saw Mandryka's hand lying on top of Julia's. He peered over the top of his glass at the pair of them. It never ceased to amaze him. What was Julia doing with such a monster? He was a regular rhino head.

—Mandryka was wondering if you'd found any investors yet? perked up Julia.

Patak set his pint down on the table and made a shape with his lips.

Mandryka took it up:

—There, Julia's reminding me. Because, as I say, I saw your presentation. And, as I say, it was impressive in many ways. I thought that if in a month or two, if you've pushed the ideas on a little further and you're still juggling with investors, not knowing what to do, you could do worse than get in touch with me back in Prague. Julia'll know how to get to me.

Patak felt an instinctive smirk powering through from the back of his throat. He let it play over his lips, but uttered no sound.

—We might talk, said Mandryka.

Patak moved his head around a little in what his American manual called active reflection.

—We might, he said after a moment or two. But a month or two is a long time in the business.

—Yes, laughed Mandryka. I know it is. I m sure you'll be in Las Vegas by then. By the way, would you mind just clarifying a little for me those force lines you talked about? The tension between audience and contestants is that they all stand to lose or gain something. Either win extra prizes or lose cash or objects from their own personal patrimony that they must put up as a stake. Am I right?

—You are, said Patak grudgingly.

—Between T.V. audience and studio audience?

—It remains to be worked out, you understand, but the T.V. audience could telephone in on a game show hotline with stakes of their own against the studio audience. The presenter would be up against the competitors. He would stand to win or lose against them.

—You could even put his two sexy assistants up against each other, interrupted Mandryka, laughing.

—Why not make them part of the stake? said Julia, turning her face away in distaste. Really, it's such a vicious view of things, Patak. Do you really think people want to play those games?

—I think they do, said Mandryka, looking at Patak in a new light as he patted him on the back and called for further drinks.

—Everybody wants to be on the wheel of triumph and defeat, said Patak, because it's so much more exotic than treading the middle road.

—I don't really see what could be so exotic about losing everything you have, said Julia.

—It's exciting because you can always reverse things, said Mandryka. Don't you see?

—Not really, she said. And anyway, how can it work out for everyone?

—It can't, of course, said Mandryka. But it's a simple redistribution of patrimony. Am I right, Patak?

Patak nodded and drank more beer.

By now Rowley was coming to the end of the Arab countries episode:

> ...Which roused my old dad, he was saying: Roused him? I'll say it roused him. He gives the Arab such a bunch of fivers that it sets him on all fours, at sixes and sevens and in two minds all at once. Stars! I'll say he saw stars! He saw more than that, Madam, he saw ruddy asteroids. Now ain't that so says I!

—Now ain't that so says I! flashed back the congregation. Patak felt their legion presence crowding in upon him.

The last he saw of Julia and Mandryka was of the two of them strolling off hand in hand like a couple of outsized Romeo and Juliets, risible, especially that monster—Patak could not get over it—with the mammoth head all obliterated and battered like a lump of old Gruyère cheese.

Patak got up and followed them a moment towards turnstiles at the end of the pier, but when he saw the iron spikes and clatter of the whole apparatus, he decided he didn't have the strength to pass through them. Instead he turned to the wooden steps that led down to the sea.

He smelt the tar from the promenade where the roadway was being re-laid. It mixed with the smell of beer and salt air. Patak had drunk too much on an empty stomach. He rubbed his stomach softly. He went down the steps towards the water, the soles of his shoes chafing gently on the wood.

Underneath the pier you could see how filthy the water was. It lapped around the legs of the pier, clanking cans against them, pushing sheets of newspaper this way and them, bobbing flotillas of cigarette butts out to sea. Patak looked forlornly out at the water. They should spend a bit more money tidying up the place he thought. It was a crying shame. They were letting the place run to wrack and ruin. It was tragic.

When he looked up he could see the activity of the pier through the lattice of the planks. Anthony Rowley was pounding on a drum. It was the death of the old dad episode:

—Woe, Madam! Woe, says I! Woe, now ain't it! Woe! Woe!

I carries the body to the crossroads.

I digs the hole to bury my old dad.

These were the hands that dug it. These were the hands.

I lays my old dad down to rest, what he'd well deserved.

I fills the hole up wit the soil and the stones.

With the soil and the stones we parts company, my old dad and I.

I breaks the staff to mark the spot.

I sheds a tear for my old dad.

Adieu, says I. Adieu and Adieu for the last time.

And when the sun came up I was gone and it was barren land again.

Patak looked out across the grey expanse of the sea towards where the clouds were shifting in. He licked the final drops of beer from his lips and went back to the Metropole. Maybe he just had the time for another look for the famous black pool before the rain set in.

## Chapter Nine: A Redistribution of Patrimony

PATAK TOOK the plane back to Prague on Saturday lunchtime. He had been away just over a week. He was coming back alone, the same man who had journeyed out there, with the same baggage, the same overcoat and under jacket, the same shoes, haircut and toilet bag. But there were new things. Undefined chromosomes of preoccupations and suspicions on the florid backdrop of his imagination were getting together, linking loops, making their allegiances known.

On Friday evening he had found the famous black pool. Or at least he thought it was the black pool. It wasn't called that now, of course. It was just a kind of dirty pond out past the football ground with a barbed wire fence round it and nothing to tell you of its history. Patak sat by it as the sun went down, a weary soul, with his armour cast off, as it were, tending his wounds after the struggle with the dragon. Here at last was peace.

Patak came in from Prague airport by taxi. The lights were coming on in the Old Town Square as he slipped obliquely past. People were going about their daily business, getting home with shopping, lights coming on in apartment windows, a doorman in the Europa Hotel was ushering guests into swing doors. Patak struggled into the lift of his block with his two square suitcases and pulled the grill behind him. He looked at himself in the oblong pane of glass of the lift door as the floors fell behind in slow motion.

As Patak travelled up in the lift, it was his wont to map out his movements for the immediate future. But now, when his mind automatically unclipped the scroll of the next few days, he saw that the parchment was virgin white.

He had no clue as to how he would occupy himself over the following days. He had no job to go back to, no friends left and the antagonisms project had all but turned to dust in his hands. He was resolving take a long bath as he was turning the key in the lock of his apartment. But even as the door was swinging open, the quality of echo from within struck him as unfamiliar.

The long green hall carpet, which usually made the bottom of the door stick, had disappeared. The door swung easily open, encountering no obstruction. The hall was empty. None of Patak's framed posters hung on the walls. A radio was playing in the kitchen. A man with ginger hair wearing an apron emerged into the hallway carrying a soup-spoon.

—Who are you? he said.

Patak doubted for a moment that he was in the right apartment.

—Patak, said Patak.

—How did you get a key? said the Gingerman and stepped one step down the hall.

—This is my apartment, said Patak.

He pulled his suitcases through into the flat and closed the door behind him. It slammed.

—No, said the man. It's already been rented, I'm afraid. I moved in here yesterday. There must be some mix-up.

—Yes. There is. This is my apartment, said Patak.

—No, said the man: I rented the apartment from the owners yesterday. I paid them three months in advance. Mr and Mrs Blackpool.

Patak's tongue was stopped. He walked up the hall and looked into the living room. It was empty. The sofa and armchairs, the low coffee table and the round dining table, the rabbit hunt rug and the sideboard with its yellow lamp: all no longer there.

Patak strode into the room. The floorboards creaked under his feet.

—What's going on? said the Gingerman.

Patak went through into the bedroom. No bed and no computer. A mattress was on the floor.

—I haven't moved my stuff in yet, said the man, as though embarrassed to be living in such conditions.

In the kitchen a panload of soup was bubbling on a two-ring hot plate. Patak turned to look at the man. The Gingerman delivered a quizzical look back. His eyebrows made a symbol Patak had once seen as a child in an algebra exercise many years ago.

Patak and the Gingerman both looked down at the bubbling pot.

—Carrot soup, explained the man.

After much discussion, with the testimony of neighbours and tradespeople from Lodski Alley at the back of Lenski Avenue—the baker stood by Patak, though the butcher after twelve years of faithful custom was unable to recognise him—the misunderstanding was resolved.

The Gingerman finally agreed to go dependent on receiving a full refund of all he had paid out to Mr and Mrs Blackpool. By 10.30 that night Patak was again alone in his Lenski Avenue apartment. He was back to square one minus his patrimony. All that remained in the apartment was a rusty old bicycle he stored in the airing cupboard. Out of a gesture of solidarity the Gingerman left his mattress and sleeping bag for Patak to sleep on that night.

Before he went to sleep Patak went down to the all night store and bought a bottle of vodka and a set of cardboard beakers. As he poured it out, midnight struck on the St Mikulase Church in Old Town Square. Patak opened up the windows and looked out to where a crescent moon winked down on him and his stone angel.

The loss of his furniture and personal effects acted as a kind of inner cleansing on Patak. He was unwilling to clutter the place after that. He bought himself a single mattress of his own, much impressed with the weekend use he had got out of the ginger mattress. That and a small folding table and a couple of hard backed chairs were his only purchases of note. Cooking was done on a camping gas canister he had picked up from a sports shop in the Novi Grad.

The telephone rang on two or three occasions over the next few days. Julia phoned to ask him how he was. He did not mention the apartment and when Julia suggested popping in on the way back from Kotva, Patak made an excuse saying he would be nipping out himself in the afternoon. Another call was from some place he'd never heard of in Germany from the pony-tailed rodent like man who had told him the presentation had been all Greek to him. It turned out that he hadn't been saying it was all Greek at all, but that the Antagonism schema reminded him of Greek tragedy with its gods, demi-gods and its ritualistic procedures. Before putting the phone down the German said he'd be in touch. Patak nodded and listened but his mind was elsewhere.

There was not a peep from Randy Hart or Lucretia. Although Patak now knew that he had been taken for a ride all along, it was still too early for him (a sluggish Capricorn with pulses of thoughtless spontaneity but great swathes of inactivity) to feel much towards them other that what he had always felt: excitement in their presence; boredom in their absence. In fact, the one thing he really missed was not being able to pick up the phone and have a chat about this and that, antagonism the idea and life in general, with Randy Hart.

When Patak quizzed himself he found there was no resentment. He had—had he not?—experienced the trip to Blackpool; the attempts to sell, to explain; he had frequented the relevant people; he had even got to see Jerzy Grotowski. Seen as a holiday or a fantasy, which was how the trip was now starting to appear to him, he had paid for it and received the goods. Hart and Lucretia, splendid tour operators that they were, had done their job. They had done a bit more besides, of course, but the disappearance, the apartment and the rest, the redistribution of patrimony as Mandryka had put it, that was all part of the thrill of the experience, the risk of spills, the spin round on the Catherine Wheel of Fortune.

Patak turned his mind away from Blackpool. Over the next few weeks, through June and into July, he engaged cautiously with one thing at a time. His first act was to cut off all communication with the outside world. He didn't want Julia asking how he was or what he was up to. He didn't answer the phone. If a call came through, the answering machine picked it up and in the evening Patak erased all messages without listening to them. Sometimes snatches of a message came through before Patak could hop into the other room. Then he found a volume switch and he was spared even the shards of disembodied voices. Now and again the doorbell rang. Patak ignored it and went on with his apartment existence.

The apartment, now bare, needed rediscovering. Its realigned contours needed massaging to meet his body, now consistently slippered and dressing gowned. He found a grocery delivery service where you paid significantly over the odds for the privilege of avoiding the holiday crowds—the shirt-sleeve season was now upon them. Exceptionally, Patak peered out into the street over the shoulder of his Angel eye, but in general he kept the heavy curtains pulled to at all times.

Patak's chief activity was sleeping. He discovered an enormous appetite for it. The second major activity was trying to perfect the art of the handstand. Also much time was spent reading labels of foodstuffs purchased via the grocery delivery service. Cereal packets were the staple text. For the first time labels came into consideration as an element to be borne in mind in the choice of foodstuff.

The arrival of the box of groceries from the delivery service was the highlight of the day. Patak struck up a rapport with the delivery man, a Mr Benn, although they kept to the contents of the delivery box for subjects of conversation. *Heavy one today*, went Mr Benn. Or else *I hope you've got a nice bottle of something in there Mr Patak*. Once Patak opened the box before Mr Benn left. The delivery man had stopped off in the bathroom before going down to the street. Patak brought milk, chocolate and rice out onto the floor. *That's done it now*, said Mr Benn. *It's Pandora's Box that is. Now I've seen what's in there, I'm not curious no more.*

Patak started to venture out. At first they were night walks up to the limits of the Karluv Bridge from where he would look across the shimmering water to the crouching silhouette of the Mala Strana. The Mala Strana was a muddy green, murky brown stretch in the early morning. Its outlines were undefined as though huge sheets had been thrown over it. In the early morning mist it looked as though hot vapours were rising from it.

After three of four night walks Patak started to venture into the Mala Strana itself. It was as though he had stored up zeal for outings and could now unleash it.

The first night he crossed over the Karluv Bridge past the sentry post for the first time, flashing his identity card at the night watchman, at two in the morning. The night was perfectly still. He heard his own footsteps ringing out on the cobblestones of the bridge. Above him on both sides the various luminary statues that adorned the parapets were little more than shadows.

Into the Mala Strana proper the night was even denser. Nobody stirred on the sloping carriageway that led up from the bridge into the heart of the district. Patak was aware of himself as a lone silhouette upon the surprisingly well-lit thoroughfare, the same thoroughfare on which he had met Randy Hart what now seemed like a lifetime ago. He passed the bean shop which was his sole landmark in the Mala Strana. It was shuttered up by a line of green planks, stacked across behind a large iron bolt. Patak walked a little further on but he did not stray from the main thoroughfare.

The next night Patak ventured down the side street where the bean shop lay. It was the first in a block of similarly boarded shops, some in rose pink, others in orange. It was in its own way picturesque. After the shops came a line of low-roofed and windowless brown houses. Patak stopped outside one of the houses and listened. From within there came a kind of low rumbling, which could have been a distant snoring or the hushed rumbling of some sort of primitive boiler. Patak turned off down another street, a narrow alleyway of the type that in his youth his mother had for some reason or other referred to as a Bluff Way. It was an impasse, lined with the same windowless brown homes, but at the very end, about one hundred paces away, set within the blank wall that stopped up the end of the cul-de-sac, the carving of a reindeer holding one of its hoofs out to a woodsman who was tending to it. As Patak was aware from his History of Prague lessons at school, the reindeer was Jesus Christ and the woodsman the City of Prague manifesting its hospitality.

He approached the carving and studied the friendly mien of the divine beast. He looked into its frank eyes and after a moment he became aware of the sound of merrymaking coming from behind the wall. It was as if the reindeer was officiating at some function and inviting Patak to partake the pleasures of what must have been a kind of all-night bar tucked at the back of the impasse.

The third night he came back to the same Bluff Way. He had still met nobody in the streets in the Mala Strana. The reindeer was still there, casting the same pleading and benign look down towards the woodsman. The same brouhaha punctuated by the odd peal of laughter came from beyond the blank grey wall.

Suddenly, with a dash and a leap and a burst of spontaneity that surprised even Patak himself, he had scrambled over the wall and found himself in another street of brown houses. However, set back from the road a little further on was a bunker-like affair called The Destroy Club.

Patak had never been a great club-goer. In fact, he had never really been inside one of these places. The first night he only stayed for half-an-hour. But the lights and noise, the bizarre dress and dance moves acted as a sufficiently alien language for him to treat the whole culture as an unengaging, uncommunicative but fascinating code to be cracked. Patak soon became fully cogniscent with the panoply of clubs available to the night bird, and undertook the outings with all the zeal of a tour round a check-list of holy shrines, The Mambo, the Zoo, the Corral, Ginas, SKY CITY, the Destroy Club. After a few nights of clubbing and a few days of sleep they all blended into one. Each club became a pinprick of light to illuminate the stretches of brown anonymity that was the Mala Strana.

In one club he became involved in a fight with a skinhead girl (either the Zoo or the Destroy Club); in another (Ginas or was it SKY CITY?) he slipped on the dance floor and ripped his trousers; after another (The Mambo or the Destroy Club?) he was invited back to a private party where he drank a kind of green cocktail and agreed (nay, volunteered) to burn his own shoes—the stench of rubber was dire; in the Zoo (or was it the Corral?) Patak spent twenty minutes kissing with a redhead before she went off to the toilet and never returned. Patak saw her two nights later in SKY CITY where he went unrecognised.

After two weeks of non-stop clubbing in the heartland of the Mala Strana club scene Patak was a wreck. He would have gone on with it too and become a fully paid up member of the club circuit, but it was too exhausting, and one early morning, on returning from a particularly exhausting night in SKY CITY, he decided to open up some mail.

One of the first envelopes he opened was from his bank. At first, he thought there was some mistake. Firstly, the habitual appellation *Dear Mr Patak* had been snipped to the ominous *Dear Client,* and what had been a Gold scheme and then been reduced to a Silver because of the Blackpool trip could now not even qualify for a Bronze. Patak's savings were gone. The imaginary graph that he plotted in his mind looked like the Blackpool Big Dipper, a terrible fall to a position where it made no sense any more.

Patak needed to stop spending money or start making it. He telephoned the Gingerman who was still looking for a suitable apartment to rent and agreed to let him the apartment for six months. Money changed hands and Patak took the train out to Pec where his mother lived in a spacious country house.

Twelve years previously was the last time he had spent a protracted period in the house near Pec. His father had died in a bizarre accident. He and Patak's mother had just moved into the house from Prague. It was intended as an idyllic country residence for their retirement. On the day the furniture arrived from the apartment in Prague, Patak's father was leaning out of the bedroom window directing the removal men in through the front door with the master wardrobe when he unbalanced and fell out of the window onto the horizontal wardrobe, which broke his fall so efficiently that five minutes later he was laughing about the incident with his wife. A thirty-foot fall from an upper storey window for a sixty-four year old and not a bone in his body broken as far as he could ascertain. *In any case,* laughed his wife, *I don't know why you were even directing the removal men in through the front door. They could see it better than you.*

*That's why I needed to lean out a bit,* laughed Patak Senior. The three removal men were by now sharing a beer and bread rolls with the jolly residents. The wardrobe, meanwhile, was somewhat the worse for wear. One of the doors was damaged and the hinges twisted by the impact.

Suddenly Patak's father felt a tickle at the back of his throat. It was his heart lurching. The funeral took place two days later. It was Patak's first sight of the house.

The house was a tall thin affair whose main feature was its ample stairs which were set at the centre of the building like a crooked backbone. The rooms, the spaces, the rest, were kind of ancillary. The stairs took up all the space, leading up to the first floor before about turning in two movements and leading up to the second floor. Halfway up each flight was an alcove with a broad windowsill overlooking the country.

After the funeral Patak decided to live with his mother in the country for a time. He had been living in Prague in student like poverty. He was not missing out on much by moving in with his mother for a few weeks.

The house was situated half way between the village and the brow of a hill. If you walked up to the top of the hill from the house—ten minutes straining along an untrodden track—you were rewarded with the four-wise view of the surrounding country. A village of salt and pepper pots, a crinkled landscape of hills and dales cut by brooks and patches of wildflower, it lay set out before you on all sides, accessible and to-hand like the contents of a large tablecloth.

After the funeral a collection of relatives and family acquaintances came back to the house. Patak's mother had called in caterers to provide a spread, which was set out in the parlour on the ground floor. There was another reception room on the first floor which was hardly differentiated from the parlour in its character. The effect was to lend an anonymity to both and to reemphasise the dominant role played by the stairs.

During the gathering guests tended to drift out of the draughty reception rooms and congregate around the stair alcoves carrying bottles of sugary wines with them. Most of the guests were banking acquaintances of the deceased whose presence at the party was little more than dutiful. They stood tall in their dark business suits at various points on the large stairway like so many dark sentinels on the dead man's life path, a life path which had been mainly a career path. They were adequately mingled with the rest but they seemed to stand above the others and were all aware of each other's presence on the stair at any one time.

After everyone had gone home Patak and his mother settled into a kind of illusory tacitly agreed routine, as though they had been living together for years. Patak spent long periods of the day at the window where his father had inadvertently defenestrated himself, looking out across the country towards the undulating hillocks.

Now and again he cast his eyes down towards the ground and followed the trajectory his fathers accelerating body had taken. The wardrobe was behind him. One of its doors had been taken off. Nothing had been put into it.

Now, twelve years later, Patak was back in the house. Patak's mother had lived alone there since the funeral. The wardrobe was still where it had been put by the removal men, still missing one of its doors, still empty. Patak's mother hardly ever ventured into the room where it stood and she had never got round to having it shifted. When Patak moved in, he stacked his clothes in there behind the single door. When he looked out of the window towards the hillocks, Patak was aware of the presence of the wardrobe at his back, very much in the same way as the stone angel had gazed with him westward over the city of Prague. The wardrobe, with the lingering presence of his dad incorporated into its wood, replaced the caryatid angel as a companion, making himself complete. The room was another displaced version of his living room in the Prague apartment, except that instead of staring gormlessly out across the onion-skin domes of old Prague, he was gawping out into the folds of Czech countryside.

Patak had never been particularly close to his father, who had been more an old-fashioned patriarch than a modern parent. When they paraded together in the streets of Prague on Saturday morning on their way to the fish market for yellow fish, they rarely spoke. It was as if Mr Patak Senior was walking the dog or showing off a new waistcoat. When they did speak the conversation turned on certain well-defined subjects: school; the vulgarity of spitting or chewing in the open street; the wonderful smell of beer from the tavern houses; the virtues of yellow fish for the skin and the immune system.

Now and again the two of them would venture out to the Sparta Prague match on Saturday afternoon, although attending the match became more and more of a bane to Patak Sr. The language he overheard at the matches was foul enough to make him visibly wince and he didn't want it falling into the portals of Patak Jr's shiny, bright ears. Patak Sr preferred the task of explaining the matrix of the league table to his son, elucidating the intricacies of the Home and Away columns and the nuances of meaning that separated goal average from goal difference. Patak sat spellbound, squeezed in between his dad's lap and the arm of the sofa, his eyes cast down onto the mass of seething numbers that was the league table.

Nowadays, Patak had very little remembrance of his father's actual features. They were kind of large and pasted onto an orb-like head, buoyant on a thick neck. Yet when he saw old photos of his dad, this mental image didn't seem to correspond to the captured reality. On the photos there was a sickly and seedy looking chap in a check sports jacket.

It was rare that Patak Sr broached directly the question of his son's future. At school Patak was a conscienscous but uninspiring pupil. In meetings with his parents, teachers found themselves unable to quite recall his face to mind. The reports they gave of him were accordingly nondescript. Patak was a bright boy who had made adequate progress although he could do much better if he put in extra effort. Patak Sr did not know quite what to make of the reports, how to direct his fatherly wisdom in a bout of advice to the offspring. This bafflement was one reason why Patak's future was rarely discussed.

Once, however, on the instigation of his wife who had gone to bed early to leave him time alone with the boy, Patak Sr tried to engage in a real conversation. Patak Sr earned a good living. He had worked his way up within the state bank in a department that dealt with financial planning. Towards the end of his career he started to earn larger sums of money, but by then his features already wore a veil of disappointment. Patak Sr had never changed jobs. In those days you didn't. It would be for his son to accomplish those many things he had not. Patak Sr poured his son a glass of beer from the large budget priced bottle and asked him what he would like to do when he left school. Patak had never really thought about it. The future was a dull, unpleasant place. He knew he was not the type to shine and would surely end up in some dreary backwater. You can do anything these days, his dad told him. This was the time when a flood of American films had been unleashed onto Czech television, all giving more or less the same message: if you really wanted to be someone, you could be—all that was really necessary was a moment of transfiguration accompanied by resurrection-style brass instruments, a close-up from camera two and a vow made to the self in splendid Technicolor, your eyes shining bright with self-realisation. If you got that far, then hop! you were home and dry as far as worldly ambitions were concerned.

His dad outlined the options: a racing driver or a businessman; a surgeon or an engine driver; a film actor or a circus trapezist. Patak was puzzled. Even to his uninformed 15-year-old mind, his dad's suggestions came across as quaint and antiquated. Not only did they betray his father's limitations in squaring up to the reality of the world of desire and ambition, but, Patak realised even then with a melancholy sigh, they also revealed to him his own limitations. For he could not be any of those things. He was not the kind to be a surgeon or a trapezist. He would end up working in an office like his dad, doing a job that films did not care about.

If Patak had ever founded any hopes in the ability of his dad to help him, he lost them then. His dad had swallowed the message of those films as something more than mere entertainment. Patak watched the loose skin around his eyes as he laboured to convince his son of the reality of the world of racing car drivers and trapeze artists. The things that Patak had taken on trust all fell away now, dissolved from his world. The merits of yellow fish were suddenly clearly illusory. Beer was fine, but it was poor man's champagne. And his dad, for all the savings he had built up, and the house he was planning to buy out in the country near Pec notwithstanding, his dad was sadly deluded about things. His dad was deluded and Patak was scuppered.

His mother was an old woman now. The activity of the house had slowed down almost to a halt. He and his mother ate one meal a day together at about five o'clock. There was little conversation. The clock ticked heavily at the back of the table. If his mother did speak her time span never stretched beyond the next day. She would remind him to bolt the door or ask him how they said the weather would turn out or tell him she had under-salted the soup. Patak too kept to these subjects.

Patak stayed there for many weeks. The idea of going back to Prague did not occur to him. One day he looked across the tablecloth landscape towards a huddle of cottages where smoke curled up from a chimney. It was winter coming back. His memory jogged and he looked over to the left for his caryatid angel. It was then that he decided to go back to Prague. Blackpool was behind him. The quiz show dream was behind him. His old mother waved him off at the station. Patak picked up on the normal trajectory of the life he was meant to live.

## Chapter Ten: The Bluff Way

LIFE resumed.

Patak took back his apartment and began the acquisition of new objects. In the Jewish quarter of the old town he found a carpet shop and acquired a rug depicting a rural scene including much threshing of hay. In a second-hand book shop near the National Theatre on Narodni Avenue he found a four-volume copy of Lives of The Romans. He equipped his living room with a broad beamed yellow sofa and a dark brown desk with a leather upholstered chair.

He found work on the in-house magazine of a financial investment consultancy, where he was responsible for lay-out and picture management. The salary was much the same as what he had been used to. He saw how there was a tacit agreement that blocked him into a specific and totally random salary tranche. It was called tranche D. He was sandwiched in there with people like Rodkey, whilst others were arbitrarily in tranche C or tranche B. Who knew why? As they say, a man's tranche is his fate.

Julia phoned and Patak agreed to have her come round. It was late morning when she got to the apartment. She was wearing one of her fetching cross-back strapped tops in emerald green and her summer lipstick.

—You've changed it in here, she said when she came into the living room.

—I had a clear-out, said Patak, gesturing to the peasants threshing hay on his rug.

—Let me make some tea, she said. I've just bought some from Mrs Orlova. It's burnt ginger and bitter orange.

Patak let her make the tea in the kitchen. He fitted himself into an angle in the kitchen woodwork and watched her resuming her familiar relationship with his crockery.

Back in the living room on the heavy masonry of the new yellow sofa, she told him how she had split up with Mandryka almost immediately on returning from Blackpool.

—It became clear to me that things were not right. He just had too much money, so he had to keep taking me places. And if I tried to take any initiatives, it was too cheap for him. It was always coming between us.

—Tragic, said Patak in a thin voice.

—No, said Julia. Of course, you're right. That wasn't the real problem. It was something I found out after we came back from Blackpool.

Julia took a sip of her tea. Patak stirred his.

—Mandryka was visiting a lady on a regular basis.

Patak's ears pricked up.

—A mistress, he said, unable to keep a triumphal element out of his voice.

Julia noticed and gave him a cold look.

—No, she said. Not a mistress, more in the nature of a hired lady.

—A harlot! blurted Patak, unable now to keep the broad grin from off his face.

—Don't use that word, please, it's so common.

—A harlot, repeated Patak. It was the perfect term for what his imagination was busy constructing.

He couldn't stop himself:

—A harlot indeed!

—Yes, yes, a harlot. Now, I say, Patak, do you have any of those Prague gingers you always used to keep?

They broke open the ginger nuts.

Over the ginger nuts there was a moment when Julia adjusted her left ear-ring, making that asymmetrical camera pose that women make when harpooning an earring right; the body stilled, the eyes intent, the two arms across on one side of the torso.

Patak watched the act he had seen a thousand times before with quiet fascination. Nobody replaced an earring quite like Julia did.

—So how did you find out about about the harlot? Patak asked later in the afternoon when they had their feet up on the new yellow sofa and he was enacting Japanese toe massage on her feet.

—He had a weekly appointment.

—And? said Patak, manipulating the second toe.

Julia smiled and unpursed her lips.

—I found out. I'd been round to his apartment once on a Friday afternoon and rang. Nobody opened, but I knew he was inside because the doorman told me he'd gone up a few minutes before. And he'd kind of winked in this funny way that got me thinking.

—What about?

—Well, his ardour... or lack of it.

Patak moved his fingers up to the big toe.

—So I went back the next week at about the same time and he opened the door, he was obviously expecting someone else, and...

Julia shook her head and smiled.

—What was it? What was it... said Patak now gripping her by the ankle.

—Well, he was got up in this kind of costume.

—What kind of costume?

—I don't know really, a bit like a Roman centurion.

—A Roman centurion.

—Yes. You know, from Ancient Rome.

—What? With the breast plate and that skirt made out of strips of stuff and the helmet and everything.

—Yes, well he wasn't wearing the helmet but I could see it on the table behind him.

167

—It must have been quite a helmet for him to get his head into it.

—I suppose so. I never saw him in it.

—Well, what was it all about?

—Well, it was kinky, wasn't it?

—Kinky?

—Yes. And then the lady arrived.

—The harlot?

—Yes. And it was obvious. I understood straight away.

—Why? What was she done up as?

—Well, she was in her coat when she arrived. So I didn't get a chance to see her costume.

Patak reflected for a moment.

—Vestal virgin probably, he said after a moment.

—Mmm, said Julia.

—What a turn-up, eh? grinned Patak. A Roman centurion, eh.

—The thing is, went on Julia, I was sure I'd seen her somewhere before, but I just can't place her.

—Maybe in one of those cards they leave in phone boxes near the Smetana Theatre. You've seen the snaps they take of themselves. Although I can't remember any vestal virgins.

—Yes perhaps, though I'm sure the vestal virgin thing was Mandryka's own invention. The one thing I can say about him is that he did have imagination.

Patak was silent and let his fingers go limp on her middle toe. He preferred not to think about Mandryka's imagination and Julia's months of exposure to it.

—The stuff he wanted us to get up to, she went on.

Patak grimaced.

—He had these games.

—Don't tell me if you don't want to. Shall I go and get some more ginger nuts? said Patak.

—No, I don't mind talking about it. In fact, it's rather nice to get it off my chest. You don't mind listening, do you?

—Of course, I don't. Why should I? replied Patak sharply.

Julia felt his unease, but went on nevertheless.

—Well, he had this game he liked to play.

—Game?

—Yes. He called it *Mandryka Says*.

Patak swallowed an unpleasant clot of saliva.

—What happened was that he said *Mandryka says do this or that*. You know.

Patak wasn't sure he did know. He looked perplexed.

—You know. Like *Mandryka says Go and make me a cup of coffee*.

—What? You had to make him cups of coffee. That doesn't sound like much fun to me.

—No. That's just an example. It was other stuff of course. You know.

She wiggled her foot at his hand.

—Saucier stuff.

—Oh, said Patak.

He looked down towards the men threshing hay.

—What. You didn't have to do the Roman Centurion stuff, did you?

—No.

—Good. Now let's go and buy some more Prague gingers, said Patak and they got up and put their shoes on.

Antagonisms disappeared from Patak's life. The heart burn that had invaded his deep throat whenever the word Blackpool was mentioned gradually diminished. He suspected that while he had been away at his mother's house, there might have been phone calls, but he could not prove it, and he rather hoped there hadn't been any. He just wanted the whole thing to go away.

Julia told him that Mandryka had mentioned the Antagonisms thing a number of times after coming back from Blackpool and had seemed interested in putting some money into the project. If Patak had been really interested he could have followed it up, but even if he had been interested, after the centurion business, Patak would have preferred to steer well clear of the Rhino head.

At night Julia sometimes told herself that something was missing from their newly reconstructed relationship. What was it? she asked herself as Patak snored in the three quarters bed beside her. The fuzzy F major chord of his computer coming on as he dived into or was it out of the window marked Antagonisms? The tugging tension that lurked at the back of all conversation, that tension being the desire to get to Blackpool or its equivalent? The inclusion of a secret passage at the back of all other life preoccupations, one labelled light entertainment?

In the end, she had been perhaps happier with Patak the boor, Patak the obsessive, forever banging on about this imaginary quiz show, which through the thick and thin of it all, she had herself constructed in her own mind, although it was sure that her version of the game differed substantially from Patak's edition. That old Patak was perhaps more fun than this new one. New Patak was present certainly in a way the old one had never been, but inhabited a rather silly space, a kind of empty vestibule that compared unfavourably with the secret passage where Old Patak had rooted about. And New Patak was up to not very much in that vestibule, talking with her about his job at the financial consultants, Leibnitz and Lisbonne, an anodyne American firm, and his confounded D tranche.

The tables were turned in that now it was Julia who looked to bring the conversation onto the old Antagonism days. What if Patak had another crack at it? Keeping money out of it, of course. But what if he at least phoned up a few of those numbers he'd picked up from Blackpool, just to see if anyone had had any thoughts on the matter? He'd given them some thinking space. Now was the time for a casual little inquiry.

But Patak was adamant on the question. It might start with a casual inquiry, but he would soon be drawn into the net and the old darkness would close in upon him again. The way Patak put it was this: There is no going back to Blackpool.

Time heals all. After a time even the sight of Chocky the Horse clip-clopping round the streets of the old town caused no more than an uprise of phlegm in Patak's throat. And very soon Julia and he were joking about it all.

Once Julia caught sight of Mandryka in an underground station near the Visurad, waiting on the opposite platform. She saw his battered face through the windows of a stationary train and was sure he hadn't spotted her. It was true he was big; a massive cannonball pudding of a head. She couldn't help smiling to see it there on display behind glass. His lips were moving slightly as though he were talking to himself. Julia imagined the thoughts whirling within his cavernous dome like dervishes, ricocheting against the walls of his cathedral cranium. When the stationary train departed, Julia slipped back behind a pillar so as not to be seen, and the next time she looked Mandryka had disappeared.

One winter—it was February—Patak was hurrying home to catch the European match on the television. Sparta Prague had drawn Manchester United in the European Champions League and the away leg was due to start at eight thirty. He had just stopped off for some bread in the grocery store Acquire and Prosper and was beginning to turn his mind to the match, when he caught sight of Randy Hart coming towards him.

It was the Randy Hart that had always been. The Randy Hart of his dreams, coming towards him smiling broadly, his hands held out in a gesture half of supplication, half of recognition, the hands somehow shapeless, more like stumps.

Before Patak could react Hart had embraced him. He held him firmly in his arms and patted him on the back a number of times. When the two of them stepped back to get a look at each other, Patak saw the degree to which Hart had changed. His face had sallowed dramatically. Patak looked for that chink of guilt or shame in his regard, but it was not there.

—How's it buzzing? Hart cried.

They were almost in the middle of the street. Patak was worrying about the proximity of traffic. He nodded a number of times by way of an answer. Patak was ashamed to be looking so much better than his former partner, who looked ravaged and poorly clad for the winter cold.

—You look great, said Hart, looking him up and down, paying particular attention to the fine woollen coat that Julia had insisted Patak pick up for the Christmas festivities. Hart was picking at it avidly with his paws.

—And how are you keeping? said Patak, having to talk to keep Hart at a distance and stop him clawing at his coat.

—Well, well, laughed Hart. Never better. How do I look?

—Fine, said Patak.

—What you see is what you get. I still get the early morning hard-on. That's the main thing, said Hart and laughed again. It's my wake-up call, he added, winking, and looking down towards Patak's crotch for some reason.

Hart took a packet of cigarettes out and offered one to Patak.

—Kepler?

—No thanks, said Patak.

Hart lit up and took a drag. He shook his head.

—Keplers, he muttered.

—And what's become of Lucretia? asked Patak for want of a better question. He just wanted this experience to be over as quickly as possible.

—I get your drift, said Hart and winked again. You mean Lucky. Remember?

Hart laughed. Patak remembered only too well.

—Oh, I don't see much of her these days. We went our separate ways in the end. It was never going to last. Too much passion either way, her and me, flame and petrol us two.

Patak nodded again as he took it in. Of course Hart and Lucretia had been a couple. How had he never realised that before? It was plain enough. And now Randy Hart wasn't even bothering to try and hide the deceit.

—Yes, he was going on. We split. And what about that quiz show of yours? How did it work out?

—Oh that, said Patak. I dropped the idea in the end. I got bored with the whole thing.

—Still, plenty more fish to fry, eh? said Hart. Listen, let me get you a drink.

—No, said Patak brusquely. I have to rush. I can't stop. I'm busy. I've got things waiting for me back home.

The truth was that the idea of a drink with Hart left him appalled.

—Tell you what. I'll drop you a line. Eh? said Hart, but Patak was already moving away.

The last he saw of Randy Hart was him standing in the gutter in his thin cloth jacket, not knowing where to go.

Patak never did see Hart again and Hart never dropped him a line.

Patak went back to Lenski Ave, where Julia had prepared a pork supper. Sparta Prague managed a draw at Old Trafford. It was 2–all with a penalty from Skolivski and an own goal from one of Manchester's lumbering centre halves, and a few weeks later in the second leg Prague won 2–1, thereby progressing to the semis for the first time in their history.

Patak's patrimony grew steadily. He never really thought about taking up the Antagonism project again, though he did receive some mail from Denmark once asking him for an update on the scheme. Patak wrote a polite letter back saying that he preferred not to undertake any further engagement at the present time. The Danish company wrote back and said they wanted to use some of his initial ideas in a new quiz show. They wanted his permission. They agreed to pay him some money.

A few months later, some cheques arrived in the post. The amounts, when transferred into Czech Crowns, were surprisingly large and ballasted his account considerably. A man from Denmark came to Prague and presented Patak with a video of the show. It was the German with the pony tail who had told him it was all Greek. He wasn't German; he was Danish. Patak settled down to watch it with Julia and the Dane. It was a good show. It was called Gambit. The host wore a devil red suit and danced about the stage set, which was a man size chess board. The audience was often spot-lit by a huge light manipulated by another man in red, although he wore a kind of boiler suit. At the back of the audience was a glass window at which were squashed the faces of another audience. This other audience seemed to be in pain, though you could not hear its screams through the wall of the glass window. They seemed to be clawing frantically at the unbreakable glass as though their very lives depended upon it. The rating figures in Denmark were apparently good.

At the end of the show Patak's name appeared. After it was written in Danish *with thanks for collaboration and inspiration.*

Two years later the show sold to America to a major network. The Danish show had written Patak into the package. Dollars would be forthcoming and it was all looking very promising. Patak's savings scheme was soon up to Solid Gold levels.

By then the Mala Strana was being renovated. It had even become a trendy area in which to invest in property. Julia agreed to a stroll along its main thoroughfare.

—Actually, she said, it's a rather charming area.

Patak took her past the bean shop, then down the side street with the low houses painted in pink and orange and brown. They were still there. Then he took her along the Bluff Way and showed her the carving of the reindeer being tended by the hospitable woodsman.

—That's Christ the Reindeer being tended by the City of Prague, he said.

—What's it doing here? she asked.

—I don't know, said Patak. But at the back of that wall there's a club.

—How do you know that? asked Julia.

—Oh, I went there a few times, said Patak.

Julia was intrigued.

—And how do you get there? she asked.

—Well, said Patak. You have to jump over the wall.

She looked at him but he seemed entirely serious.